# TOO AFRAID TO LOVE YOU

A Novel by

Renee

*Copyright © 2020 L. Renee Bazile*

*Published by Major Key Publishing*

*www.majorkeypublishing.com*

**ALL RIGHTS RESERVED.**

Any unauthorized reprint or use of the material is prohibited. No part of this book may be reproduced or transmitted in any form or by any means, electronic, or mechanical, including photocopying, recording, or by any information storage without express permission by the publisher.

This is an original work of fiction. Names, characters, places and incidents are either products of the author's imagination or are used fictitiously and any resemblance to actual persons, living or dead is entirely coincidental.

**Contains explicit language & adult themes suitable for ages 16+**

To submit a manuscript for our review,

email us at

submissions@majorkeypublishing.com

### Acknowledgments

Thank you, Q. Nicole for giving me the chance to share my stories.

Thank you to my family, Juke, Chris, and Ya for being patient with me as I tap each story out, all while attempting to function as a normal mother and wife. I know I'm not normal, lol. I love you.

Thank you to anyone who downloads a copy of this book. Please allow my words to take you places and introduce you to things you won't soon forget.

Here it goes…Book One of what might become a trilogy… Temple and Cairo- Too Afraid to Love you

**Intro…**

It doesn't matter how far I travel away from home; I will always be daddy's little girl. My dad and my brothers will go out of their way to protect me. Of course, protecting me has become more of a challenge since I decided to pack up my things and move over a thousand miles away from my family. The job opportunity from Apryl Simmons, the owner of a Fortune 500 company, seemed like a once in a lifetime opportunity. Rather than be filled with regret, I knew I had to jump on it. It would have been hard to go if both my mom and dad didn't give me their blessing. My two big-headed older brothers packed my things into a moving truck and drove me to California themselves. Even they looked reluctant to leave me alone to fend for myself.

Now it's just me and the brown girl, I call Becca, from work. Becca has become like the sibling I'd never had. Growing up, being the only girl besides my mom in the house has had its ups and downs. As the only girl besides my mom in the house, it never seemed anyone could relate to me. People have always told me I am a replica of my mother with smooth, Mocha brown skin, untamed, long black hair, and the figure of a goddess, with curves stacked to a weight of about 180 pounds. My father spoiled me so much I have often wondered if my mother resented having a little girl. Of course, he spoiled my mother as much as he spoiled me. He just went out of his way to make sure I knew how I should be treated.

If my father and brothers knew the way Aaron had been disrespecting me this past year, they would no doubt have his head. And I mean that literally. I went to bed last night waiting for his call to let me know he was outside. But the call never came. The fact that I know there is someone else should be enough for me to send him packing out of my life, but I've been hesitant because I don't want to be alone. Becca keeps telling me that I have everything I need in her until the man who will sweep me off my feet comes along. It looks like I am going to be better taking her up on that offer. When my phone lights up with Becca's name across the screen, I answer with a smile.

"Hiiii."

"Hey girl, are you going out tonight?" her high-pitched voice bubbles over my line. It's Friday night, and normally, I step out for a few hours to socialize. Or better yet, be seen in public. According to Apryl Simmons, you never know who may be watching. She wants her company to stay on the tips of people's tongues. And in this last year, most people associate me with Apryl's company even more so than Becca, who has been working with Apryl for almost five years. Becca doesn't mind it being that way. She prefers to remain behind the scenes of everything if she can.

"Yeah, since you insist that I go with you tonight, I guess I am," I reply teasingly.

"Well then, be ready in an hour."

"Alright, see you in an hour."

Our regular hangout spot on the boardwalk is a quaint corner location right between a hookah bar and a tattoo parlor. Foot traffic is quite a bit, but we both love the atmosphere and the different people walking along the strip. Most of the people who frequent the bar are college students and professionals like me who are just looking to relax a little.

After hanging up the phone, it only takes me a few minutes to decide on a black mini dress, paired with strappy black sandals that lace all the way up my calf. Taking my hair out of my signature bun, then curling it to frame my face only takes ten minutes. I apply a light and natural coat of makeup to my face to make it appear that my skin is glowing. I am one of those women who only applies makeup on the weekend and for special occasions. And tonight might be one of those special occasions. I have been expecting a call from Aaron; our night of passion is long overdue. Just thinking of the things he has done to my body make my belly quiver.

By the time I am done with my hair and minimal makeup, Becca has sent me a text message to let me know she is waiting outside for me. Taking one last look in the floor-length mirror in my hallway before I step onto the elevator, I smile at my reflection. I hope tonight will be the night I come back to my loft apartment to find my boyfriend waiting outside with a smile and an engagement ring to finally let me know he is ready to settle down with me. I've been patiently waiting for this last year.

As I approach my friend's car, she howls at me. "Damn, girl. You're putting it all out there tonight, aren't you?" she looks at me with her thick eyebrows raised well above her stylish glasses.

"Umm, no ma'am. You act like I'm naked, Becca."

"Hummph," she grunts as she watches me slip into the passenger seat of her car. When I tug at the hem of my skirt to cover a little more of my thick thighs, I chuckle to myself. This little mini dress is a little shorter than my usual. However, it's comfortable, so I don't even give a second thought to changing.

"Are you sure you don't want to change into something a little less revealing?"

"I'm okay." When I smile at my friend devilishly, she shakes her head at me before backing out of the parking space in front of my loft apartment.

Becca is a little on the conservative side. Anything risqué would make her blush. She should know me by now, I push envelopes but keep it classy all the time.

She is dressed in her usual capris, tank top, and slides. When we go out together, I am never surprised that this is her attire. We step into the bar chattering about the day's events at the office. Our boss, Apryl Simmons, had been nominated as one of the most successful women of the year. The fact that she has her hand in quite a few projects, which has made her business grow to large numbers in such a short period of time, has gotten the company a lot of recognition. Her hard work is beginning to pay off and I couldn't be prouder to be a part of her team. I suppose Becca and I should deem tonight as celebratory.

As soon as I step to the bar, someone is sending me a drink. Before I can fix my mouth to thank the stranger for the drink but decline it, my smoky lidded eyes fall upon my soon to be ex-boyfriend Aaron, who is sitting in a booth with some girl on his lap. From the looks of it, it doesn't look as if he minds the extra weight from her making him a seat. Becca turns her head to see what has grabbed my attention.

"Oh, he is bold as hell, isn't he?" she whispers loudly

with a frown on her face.

Becca lightly grabs my hand, as soon as I begin to walk toward the booth they are seated in.

"Girl, don't even go over there."

"Oh no. This time, I will not walk away quietly."

She follows me as I walk away from her. When I am standing directly in front of Aaron and his little entourage, my thoughts are heavy with the memory of the late-night phone calls that he tries to discreetly silence when he spends the night with me. My drive comes from growing tired of pretending I don't see his mess. There have been mysterious text messages he has tried to hide and then random disappearances. All these things have gotten old, and I know I deserve better. Walking over to the booth where they are seated, I hear one of his friends whistle under his breath while looking at me.

Aaron, my boyfriend, is too preoccupied with looking down the woman's open button-down, which reveals the top of her lush breasts. She has her head thrown back against his shoulder as if they are the only two people in the booth when there are four more people besides them.

Without giving a second thought to interrupting them, I wet my lips with the tip of my tongue before allowing my voice to wash over his ears.

"Well, good evening, Aaron."

He looks up at the sound of my voice, then damn near knocks the girl off his lap when he looks up to see me standing in front of the booth. But it's too late; he has been caught philandering. And at this point, there is no way he can tell me I have witnessed anything different. The slender woman looks at me with a frown, so I smile at her even though she is the one who is in violation of what I know as my relationship with Aaron.

Just from dealing with the ex-girlfriends and now wives of my brothers, I know this woman in front of me doesn't know any better. Aaron probably told her he is single or looking for a way out of our relationship as if he has shackles on his ankles. This woman may not know any better, so I ignore the ill expression on her face and continue to address Aaron.

"So sorry for the interruption, what I have to say will take less than a minute. Aaron, I will place your things on my doorstep tonight. You have until tomorrow morning to get them off or I will call a charity to come pick them up as a donation."

"Temple, it's not what you think, I-I-" Aaron scoots out of the booth with his hands up like he is under fire and I am the one holding the weapon. Although I am surprised by his defense, I cut him off with a smile and an even tone of voice.

"It's exactly what I think. And you know you don't need to explain anything." As I turn to walk away from the booth, I can hear the loud whispers of his friends behind me.

"Damn Aaron, baby girl has thick thighs for days. Who did you say she is again?" one voice says.

"Haven't you heard the saying thick thighs save lives. You better throw that dry ass breast back and go get them thighs." Another one chuckles, causing them all to laugh at the other woman's expense. In that moment, I am proud of having well-toned, thick thighs as a result of visiting the gym for an hour every day of the week except one.

When Apryl Simmons told me she wanted the world to know who I am, I decided to make sure I would be one assistant they wouldn't forget seeing. Yet, tonight, in this very moment, I wish I could disappear into my own apartment. Just as I reach the bar again with the intention of ordering a drink to settle my emotions, I hear a voice behind me. "You're a dumb bitch for coming in here trying to cause a scene all because the boy doesn't want your washed-up fat ass." When I turn around to see who the voice belongs to, a great rush of liquid and cold hard ice slams into my face. The liquid is beer, and now it has drenched the front of my dress, my face, and even my hair. I'm a timid girl, yes, but not tonight.

"Are you crazy?" I say more to myself than to her as I move toward her. Just as I move, Aaron rushes to grab the girl by her waist. He pulls her just out of my reach.

"I can't believe you're in here embarrassing yourself."

"Get off me. It's all your fault, you two-timing bastard! Let me go!!"

The burly security guard, who has been standing at

the door, approaches Aaron.

"I'm going to have to ask you to leave."

"You need to tell her that," The chick with Aaron has the nerve to say.

The man shakes his head at her, "You just threw a drink on this woman. I need you to leave."

"Come on, let's go."

The woman cusses and fusses as Aaron carries her out of the bar. Leaving me standing there humiliated, again. "Here you go, sweetheart." A guy with a familiar face, who is seated at the bar holds out a napkin. I consider rolling my eyes at him, but that would be foolish of me. My ill feelings are toward Aaron and his little friend, not toward this stranger. "Thanks."

Taking the napkin from him, I dab at the beer dripping from the front of my body. It's useless to stand here and try to dry off. My night has been ruined, and I need to go home. Just as I turn to look for Becca, who had only left me for a minute, she comes walking up to me, looking confused.

"Are you okay? What the hell did I miss?"

"I'm ready to go."

Tears burn the back of my eyes as I turn away from Becca, only to lock eyes with the familiar stranger seated at the bar. When he raises his glass of, what looks like bourbon at me, I feel something strange that causes me to look away.

"Yes, girl. Can you believe that winch threw her cheap ass drink on me?" My tone is nonchalant. Even though I am embarrassed right now, and my heart is in my throat, I manage to change my tone because I remember who I represent each time I go out.

"Damn, are you going to press charges for assault?" My coworker looks at me with pity, making me feel even more ashamed. Her question is innocent, and I know she means well.

"No. not this time."

My friend raises her eyebrows at my admittance. Of course, I wanted to cry on someone's shoulder about the amount of disrespect I have had to deal with these last couple of months. But I'm beyond embarrassed about it. After bringing this man over a thousand miles to be with me, he disregards my feelings like I don't mean anything to him. My mother warned me, yet I didn't listen.

"I'm sorry, Temple."

"Don't be sorry, girl. Be happy for me. He showed me exactly what I needed to see. So now I can move on."

"You know you loved his dirty draws," she jokes, causing us both to laugh. I know my friend is trying to make light of the moment. Because indeed, it is way too heavy for a Friday night. But I must face it. It is what it is. Aaron has proceeded to play in my face as if he had been playing a game of chess the whole time he has been here with me.

"Not hardly." Is my reply as I blink back tears of humiliation. I had believed in Aaron. When he shared with me that his parents told him he'd always be a failure, I told him they were wrong, and I would be the one to show them they were. Instead of allowing him to find his own way after I gave him an invitation to join me, I did what most lonely, affection-starved people do. I sent him a plane ticket, one way out of VA. Having asked myself a thousand times has it been worth it, while Aaron has had a field day at my expense literally. And trying to hide it from my family has been easy, considering Aaron and I don't live together.

My father had instilled in me the belief that a man won't respect a woman he can enjoy all the convenience of living together without putting a ring on her finger. To say the least, Aaron still doesn't respect our relationship.

When Apryl needed me to work late, it would be Becca and I pouring coffee while taking notes. Attending last minute phone conferences and setting up important meetings so often it prompted Becca to make the comment that I couldn't have a man with the hours that I'd put in.

"So, I guess you don't have one either."

"Your observation is correct, sweetheart. I'd rather have plenty of money to go shopping than to have a man play with my feelings." At first, her words hit me hard in the chest, causing my heart to swell in my chest cavity, coupled with the pride I have left. She and I stared at each other. I am unsure if the harshness of the reality should be taken as a joke or an insult. Within a few seconds, I decided not to take her words to heart. First of all, she doesn't know enough about me, so taking it as an insult only says the truth has slapped me in the face, and I want to take it out on someone.

"I guess you're right."

With my pride tasting bitter on my tongue, I made a new friend.

In the days that followed, Aaron called me so often I ended up blocking his number. When I started to receive calls from odd numbers, I decided to change my number altogether. I am determined to never let him know how much my feelings are hurt. When the weekend is over, I show up to work with a smile on my face like I hadn't been crying over this half ass relationship all weekend.

The morning has been filled with meetings with one contractor after another

As I am preparing for a two o'clock appointment with a new contractor, my boss, Apryl Simmons, steps into my office. She has pushed her silver-rimmed reading glasses on top of her beautifully coiffed hair. "It's just Monday," she lets out a deep breath before clasping her hands together. "Okay, so I have been mulling over this plan all day."

"What plan is that?"

"My plan to approach Cairo Evans with this expansion of our new urban housing development. If I get Mr. Evans on board, we will be able to build so many more affordable living spaces for the working class and impoverished."

"I'm excited about this project as well. Did you get those numbers I researched?" Her reveal surprises me and excites me at the same time. She clasps her perfectly, manicured hands together as she smiles at me.

"Yes, looking at those numbers, helped make my decision to approach this man. I feel like if people are given more affordable options, it'll be an incentive for them to do everything they can to maintain it. These communities need to see someone going to bat for them."

"I agree. When are you going to approach Mr. Evans?"

"His assistant has been in contact with me about chatting with him over dinner."

"Hmmm." A little birdie named Rebecca had shared with me all about the fetish Apryl Simmons has for younger men, especially the one named Cairo Evans. Becca has revealed to me more than once the conversations she has overheard our boss having about Cairo.

"Business first, always. The time that he suggested is the only time soon that Mr. Cairo Evans will be available."

"So, the date has been set?"

"The business dinner has been set for Saturday evening."

"This Saturday evening?"

"Yes, soon. After that, he is going to be out of town for several weeks. That's why I had to jump on the date."

"Thanks for sharing. Is there anything you want me to prepare for you? Is there any more research that needs to be completed before Saturday?" I am eager to make sure everything goes off without any problems. Apryl removes her glasses from her head then places them over her eyes,

"What you have gathered is great. The information you were able to compile is more than enough. If I haven't told you already, thank you for all your hard work."

"No problem, Ms. Simmons."

Apryl leaves me and Becca to come up with several scenarios about how her dinner meeting with Cairo Evans could end.

## Cairo

Nothing has come easy for me. I mean nothing. My father made sure of that. When I turned 17, my father finally took me under his wing. Earl Evans made sure I worked for every penny I earned. From working out in construction to making sure materials were received in his business. Some may look at me and say, I was blessed with a silver spoon in my mouth just because of who my father is. He is a self-made millionaire with his hands in construction, top of the line technology and even pharmaceuticals. When I hear someone say I was born with a silver spoon in my mouth, I would kindly correct them by saying I had a silver spoon on the table. By saying that I mean, nothing was ever given to me.

These last few years have been tough. After saving my little sister from the clutches of a ruthless drug dealer that only had access to her because of my mother, who had turned into a crack fiend, my life has finally returned to normal. I have been handling my business with an iron fist. Evans Construction has become one of the most highly sought after companies for new projects. My name is on numerous apartment buildings, bridges, new roads, and office buildings, just to name a few things. I have been able to accomplish a lot for my people to be proud of.

As I'm sitting on my balcony looking over the lake, my ringing phone breaks me out of my moment of reflection. My assistant reminds me of the business dinner with Apryl Simmons.

"I didn't exactly agree."

"I understand, but this will be good for publicity. You do understand you have okayed this new project and you need support?"

"Now hold on, I don't need anything." I correct her.

"I'm sorry, you're right. However, it will look good to be seen in public with Apryl Simmons."

"As long as you make sure she knows I'm not interested in a partnership."

My assistant sighs before saying, "Just show up, listen to her plan. Tell her you think it's a good idea and that you will think about the possibility of."

"Stephanie." She knows I am seconds away from

debating and shutting her completely down.

"Have I ever steered you wrong, Mr. Evans?"

"No, Stephanie, you have not."

"Okay. Well, trust me on this."

"Alright, send me the reservation details, and I will be there."

"Will do." As soon as I disconnect the call with Stephanie, I receive a call from my little sister.

"Yes, Ivory?"

"Ro, when are you coming to get me?" She is the only one besides my mother who can call me by my nickname and not get ignored.

"Your break doesn't begin until next week."

"True, but I don't have any exams the rest of this week. I'm ready to come home."

"Ivory, you do know I am running a business, don't you?"

"It's your company, so you can do whatever you need to do."

"Ivory, you are spoiled."

"I miss you, Ro. I miss my own room, my own space,

my own things. I'm tired of it here."

Her admission immediately melts my heart. And as always, I become putty in her hands.

"I'm coming to get you in the morning. Now my schedule is tight. I expect you to have everything together when I get there." I am mentally calculating everything I need to do in the next twenty-four hours. Before now, it didn't include taking a detour to get my little sister, but I promised whenever she called, I would come.

"Okay, Ro. I love you."

"I love you too, Ivory. See you tomorrow."

## Stephanie

Cairo Evans hasn't been easy to work for, but I have been working hard for this man for five years. When he started this company, he admitted he had no idea what he was doing. He only wanted to show his father that he could run a profitable business. My close friends told me I am a fool for even considering working for him. I knew I was taking a big chance that he would fail, and I would fail right along with him.

For the last five years though, this man has put in so much work, gotten so much money, and so much recognition I feel like I have struck a gold mine. When he was recognized as an entrepreneur to watch in the Fortune 500, I thought he would recognize me. But he hasn't. Anything he comes at me with is about business and business only. I should be happy with my growing credentials, but nothing would make me happier than to have him as my prize. I feel like we have built this company together. No monetary compensation will ever compare to the feelings I have for him. Cairo just doesn't know it. Hanging up the phone, I thumb through my contacts to find the number of a friend of mine. He is a restaurateur of a fine restaurant in midtown.

"Hey, Jerry, this is Stephanie. I need a favor."

"What's that, Stephanie?"

"I need to make reservations for Mr. Cairo Evans and a guest."

"When?"

"Tomorrow night."

"Sweetheart, everything is booked."

"Make an exception for me; I know you save two tables."

"Stephanie, this is last minute."

"I know, I know. I'm sorry. I really need to make this happen for my boss."

After a long pause and a little paper shuffling in the background, my friend's voice finally comes over the line, "No later than seven thirty. He needs to be here. Do you understand?"

"Yes, I understand. Thank you so much, Jerry. How can I repay you?"

He grunts. "Just make sure Mr. High and Mighty

Cairo Evans walks through that door by seven thirty tomorrow night."

After thanking him once more, I hang up the phone then sit down to my laptop to send Cairo and Apryl Simmons an email about the reservations. I also include a short agenda for the evening. When I am satisfied that my work is done for the evening, I go to my bathroom and start a warm bath for me to relax in while I sip a glass of wine.

**Aaron**

Since last night I have been constantly calling Temple's phone. Now she has changed her number, and the only way I can contact her is if I show up at her apartment or her job. I know I have messed up majorly this time and there will be no just walking back into her life as if nothing has happened. Since the day I met her, I have known I should have stepped back because I'm not ready to settle down. But when I met Temple, I couldn't walk away without saying something to her. I will never say she is out of my league, because we have shared some very deep conversation about politics, life, spirituality, and her job.

She has convinced me that if I couldn't keep up with her conversation, then I didn't belong in her conversation. She makes me consider slowing down. No more strip clubs, raunchy hotel parties and secret meetings with women. Temple deserves to be my only one. Especially after seeing the hurt on her face when she saw me with some random chick that doesn't mean anything to me.

Temple is tough, so she hid the hurt and disappointment very well. Everybody else with me keeps saying how mad she was, but I know her well enough to see through her mask. If I can just apologize to her, I think I may have another chance with her.

## Temple

For most of the day, it has been business as usual until it was time for lunch. Today I had planned to go out to have a late lunch at a diner across the street from the office. Apryl and I had been in several meetings since 9 a.m. and we have one more to get through before we're able to call it a day. My plan is to grab a quick bite then run right back into the office for the last meeting of the day. Crossing the street, the first thing I notice is the familiar walk of a man coming toward me. The last person I want to see is Aaron, and just like my luck, he is approaching me. The first thing I do is hold up my hand to stop him from talking.

"Look, I'm busy. I don't have time to listen to anything you have to say."

"Baby, I understand you are mad at me about what you saw. I promise you it didn't mean anything."

"Mad?"

Shaking my head, I take a step back so he can see the look on my face. How badly I want to correct him by telling him that I wasn't mad, I was hurt. But instead of wasting my breath to explain the difference, I roll my eyes.

"If it didn't mean anything, Aaron, then why did you do it?" When I feel the heat rise to my cheeks, I decide to take a step back. "You know what? I really don't even care. Let that woman, girl or whatever she is to you, see about you."

Now, I'm debating on getting in my car and going across town for lunch since I have an hour and a half to burn before the meeting.

"Temple, it was nothing."

"So are you and I, Aaron."

The words sound weird coming from my mouth, but I know it's for the best.

When he hears the finality in my tone, I can see him take a step back. Aaron has always been a confident guy. In fact, the moment he steps into my space, he had his shoulders squared, as he stands with his back straight and his feet spread apart. The man should be given an award for his stance alone. But, right now, I am believing he is now as unsure of himself as he is of me. Now that I have completely lost my appetite, I begin to walk right past the door of the diner toward the parking garage where I parked my car.

"Temple, please forgive me, bae. I'm sorry."

Aaron hadn't called me bae in a long time. Hearing the pet name he had given me reminds me of how much I have missed his touch.

"You have said you're sorry before. You're in no way sorry if you keep doing what you claim to be sorry for."

Tears threaten to push forward, making me blink several times. Just a minute ago, my body was stiff and braced for a fight. But now the fight has tiptoed in the opposite direction. Leaving me foolish and vulnerable in this second. He can sense my resolve, just like a predator can smell the fear of his prey. Aaron is close enough to touch me, so when he extends his arm, his fingers sweep across my skin, causing goose pimples to break out on my arms.

When I don't move, he takes that as permission to step completely into my space. Aaron places his finger beneath my chin to angle my face up so that I am looking into his dark brown eyes.

"I love you, bae. Forgive me."

Although, *"you're stupid if you let him back in"* is in the back of my mind. I allow him to pull me into his arms. With his arms completely around me, I inhale his sensually enticing cologne and become hypnotized. As soon as I drop my head to his chest, I feel my cell phone vibrate in my pocket. Saved by the bell- I breathe with relief.

"I need to get back to work."

"But you were going to have lunch." Unexpecting of my sudden detachment, he looks confused.

"I need to get back to work."

As quickly as I can, I step out of his embrace then begin to walk back toward the pedestrian crossing.

"Temple, can I come see you tonight?" he calls after me.

His question causes me to smirk a little, because he almost had me. This question reminds me that he can't be sorry if he has continued to disrespect me. His typical question receives no answer from me as I make my way safely across the street. Leaving him standing there looking after me. As I cross the street, I pull my cell phone out to see that there's a call from Becca.

"Hey."

"Girl, where are you?"

"I'm coming into the building now, is something wrong?"

"Apryl is sending you to have dinner with Cairo Evans. Her kid fell at daycare, and she had to leave. The doctors say he broke his arm."

"What? How in the hell did he break his arm at daycare where they are supposed to be watching him?"

"Apryl was livid, because she wants to know the same thing."

It takes a few minutes for it to register what Becca has just said before telling me about Apryl's kid. So, it takes a minute before I ask her to repeat what she just said.

"Hold on, did you say she is sending me to have dinner with him? Oh no, I'm not even prepared for that today."

"You better get prepared. She emailed me the

reservation details along with a copy of the agenda that his assistant proposed." When I don't say anything right away, Becca adds, "Apryl is counting on you tonight."

If I don't know anything else about my boss, I know she counts on me for a lot of her successful meetings with lenders and other potential clients. After several seconds Beck calls out to me. "Are you there?"

"I don't have anything to wear." Clothing has never been an issue for me. Even when I don't go out, I shop for the latest and greatest threads to put on my body, even if I am just going to the bar or to catch a movie alone.

"Get it together, Temple. What can I do to help you?"

Now my nerves have bundled at the pit of my stomach. As I take a deep breath to calm my nerves, I look toward the ceiling.

"Help me find something to wear."

"The last meeting is in 30 minutes. Why don't we leave right after to head to the strip?"

"Sounds good," I respond as I push the door open to my office. My mind is in a mess, of course. I'm not ready to meet the man I have seen at special events for the likes

39

of him and the woman who employs me.

## **Cairo**

The ride to get my little sister Ivory went by quick enough. Ordinarily, I would take the trip in my private jet, but when I got up this morning, I felt like taking the ride in my truck. Ivory had just gotten her license, so I let her drive the three hours back. Since we have been back at my home, she hasn't put down her cell phone, and she has barely come out of her room.

When I moved into this mini mansion two years ago, I had considered it too big. Now that I have custody of my sister and she has come to live with me, this seven-bedroom, five-bath house is plenty. When she isn't in school, Ivory occupies the rooms on one side of the house while I have my peace on the other side.

My assistant, Stephanie, has been calling my phone all afternoon. When I finally answer, she wants to know if I'm ready for the dinner with Apryl Simmons. And I have no desire to go.

"Look, can't we cancel?"

"No, Mr. Evans. It wouldn't be a good idea to cancel. Again, this is about publicity. I have already contacted some of my friends in the media, who have agreed to cover this dinner."

"I'm not interviewing with anyone tonight Stephanie."

She sighs in exasperation.

"Right, you will not be interviewing with anyone tonight. You will be sitting down to have dinner with Apryl Simmons. During this dinner, you will listen to her discuss her new project. When dinner is over, you will tell her that your team will be in touch with her soon. Now I have made this thing simple. All you need to do is show up. Look at the agenda I sent to you, just a brief look. Arrive at the restaurant at seven fifteen."

"Alright, Stephanie. I trust you on this one."

"Have I ever let you down?"

"Not yet."

When my little sister comes bouncing past me with her cell phone plastered to her ear, I reach out to snatch it from her. She looks at me with widened eyes as I place the phone to my ear and tell her little buddy she will call them back later. I don't even know if it is a male or female on the other end of the phone. And of course I don't care.

"Ro?" she wines.

"Ivory," I mock her. "Get off the phone long enough to help me find something to wear for this business dinner tonight."

Her eyes light up as she extends her hand. "Yes! You want me to go shopping?"

"Hell no."

I hear her kiss her teeth as she places her hands on her hips then pops her gum loudly.

"How am I going to help you find something to wear if you don't want me to shop for you?"

"I have plenty of clothes to choose from."

"Where?"

She looks as if she doesn't believe me, causing me to laugh. "Follow me."

I lead her to my side of the house, where I have a bedroom closet designated for my business suits and such. A large executive chair sits behind the large oak desk where I sit to handle any business that wasn't handled at my office. Across from my desk is a large, mahogany colored winged back chair. All the bookshelves that line the walls are filled with so many books you would think I went to school to study law or something. The interior designer I had hired told me she mastered creating illusions. And I can say that is the truth. You'd never guess I hadn't so much as touched any for these books.

"Okay, Ro, this looks like a big ass office. I don't see any clothes in here."

"Watch your mouth, girl. The clothes are in that closet." I point, wondering how she has the audacity to use profanity around me. She pulls the closet door open to reveal the designer suits hanging on racks and the shoes lining the bottom of the closet.

"All this stuff is boring. It looks the same. What kind of dinner are you going to and who is going to be there? If you are trying to impress somebody, you aren't going to do it with these pieces in here. I mean."

Frowning, she pushes the clothes with her fingers.

"It's a business dinner."

44

"Okay, who is going to be there?"

"Apryl Simmons."

"Okay, who is she?"

"She is a colleague. She wants to partner with me on a building project."

"So, she is the one who needs to be trying to impress you, I guess."

"Impress me for what? This is business."

"Whatever, Ro. I don't know too much about your business, but I think if you are going to have a business dinner with a woman, you need to go in like you are after her panties."

Her explanation catches me completely off guard.

"You should be learning about my business."

"For what? I am not the heir to your father's fortune."

"But you are the heir to mine."

Ivory suddenly gets quiet again. She begins to riffle through the suits in my closet, seemingly dissatisfied with each one she put her hands on.

"Why are you so quiet?"

"I don't know, Ro." While I am talking to her, her

fingers are gliding over the screen of her phone.

"You really need to think about it."

"Umhumh, where are your shirts?"

My little sister must think I am joking when I say she is my heir. Everything there is to know about this business, I want her to know. She has been taking classes in real estate and business on top of her normal course load in school. Ivory has a bright future ahead of her, and I have made it one of my top priorities to make sure she knows this.

She also has an eye for fashion. By the time I am dressed and ready to go to dinner, Ivory has pulled from my closet items that I have worn only once or twice to make them into a brand-new outfit. I have never been into designer clothing, yet when I let my little sister splurge at the mall, she has come back with a few pieces for me. Tonight, I am stepping into the restaurant wearing Ferragamo loafers paired with black slacks and blazer by Armani. She chose a pale blue button down with no tie. To say the least, I feel a little uncomfortable not wearing a tie. But my sister insists, "This is an informal business dinner, correct?"

"I guess so, Ivory."

"What do you mean, you guess? I looked at the restaurant ratings and I see it's not stuffy and upscale. So, you don't have to be stuffy like you are in an upscale environment. Just relax. I also checked out Apryl Simmons. She is truly a sista about her business, but she is not a stiff one. Don't expect her to show up in an evening gown or a power suit." The way Ivory is doling out instructions makes me look at her twice. She could surely give my assistant Stephanie a run for her money when it comes to finding out things she needs to know how to move. Before I can ask her questions, she is sending me out the door with a reminder that I need to be at the restaurant in less than thirty minutes.

The drive is short, I immediately assume Stephanie purposely made sure the restaurant is close by my residence. And to top it off, when I give the hostess my name, she takes me right back to a table that has been set for two. Just as I sit down, I look up to see a tall woman with the skin the color of mocha and piercing, slightly slanted eyes seemingly, gliding toward me. My first inclination is that the hostess she is following will walk right past this table. Picture my mouth almost dropping when she stops where I am sitting. This woman is not Apryl Simmons.

"Good evening, I am Temple Harris, Apryl Simmons' assistant. She sends her apologies for not being able to make it at the last minute." Ordinarily, I would be pissed, because I felt like Apryl has no regard for my time by standing me up. However, this young woman standing in front of me stands as a welcome substitute. As I get up to pull out her chair, no words have come to me just yet, until I step close to her and get a whiff of the light scent of her perfume.

"Temple Harris, I am glad you could make it on her behalf."

A slow smile spreads across her lips and I swear I catch a little twinkle in her eyes. It almost seems like I have met her before or at least been in the same room with her before. But where? The whole time she is talking to me, presenting the facts about Apryl Simmons' project.

I hear her, but I am also thinking of where I have met her previously.

## Stephanie

It is now nine a.m. and I expect the business dinner to be over. Just before Cairo is due to arrive at the restaurant, I receive a message from Apryl Simmons' assistant. When I learned that Apryl couldn't make it because of a family emergency, I expected Cairo to be pissed. Working as his assistant for the last five years has been enough time to get to know him. He would feel that Apryl has no regard for his time after he made time to see her.

Now I have sent him at least two text messages, and I have left him just as many voice mails. When he finally answers, I feel a weight lifted from my shoulders, "Mr. Evans, I'm sorry I didn't get with you to let you know Ms. Simmons couldn't make it-"

Before I could explain, he cuts me off. His tone is totally nonchalant, and it catches me off guard.

"It's quite alright."

"No, Mr. Evans, I need to apologize. You changed your plans to attend this dinner tonight."

"Stephanie, calm down, it's alright. Her assistant

showed up."

Looking at the phone, I try to decide if I am glad he doesn't seem to be upset. Sometimes when Cairo Evans is upset about something, he can be the worst person to work for. It's at those times when I want to call him everything that isn't his name. But at the same time, I get this foreign feeling at the pit of my stomach.

"Are you there?"

When his deep voice creeps into my little reverie, I clutch my stomach.

"Yes, I'm here. I'm glad to hear someone showed up. Now you can remove the task of meeting Apryl Simmons from your list. Now that the task is done, we can move on to your next project."

Cairo clears his throat, "You know, Ms. Simmons proposal was quite impressive. The way the project was conveyed in the agenda didn't do the actual project any justice. I'd like to-"

This time, I cut him off.

"Wait one minute. Hold on, you'd like to what?"

"I'd like to learn more. Possibly get involved."

His change of heart floors me. Just days ago, when I approached him about the meeting to begin with, he was very reluctant to meet with Apryl Simmons.

"Okay, uhh-"

"Set up another meeting."

"Why, yes. I will contact Apryl to find out when she is available."

He clears his throat again before speaking, "A meeting with her assistant will be fine."

"Mr. Evans, what changed your mind?"

The line is quiet for a few moments. During that little period of time, I find myself biting my nails. "It's for a good cause."

Slowly, I nod my head as if Mr. Evans is standing in front of me.

"Okay." It's my job as his assistant to make things happen. As I hung up the phone, I make a conscious decision to make things happen. This time I will make an extra effort to make sure he sees all that I am willing to do for him.

## Aaron

It's almost ten p.m., and I have been posted up outside of Temple's apartment for at least an hour. Glancing at my watch, I see that it is almost ten p.m. It's a little later than usual for her to be getting off work. Automatically, I begin to wonder what she is doing coming in at this hour. From where I have strategically parked my car in the parking lot, I can see that she isn't dressed in her normal office outfit either. Temple looks as if she has just come in from a date. The porch light that illuminates her face highlights her makeup, causing me to become even more worried about where she could have been.

The last thing I want Temple to do is to start seeing someone else. This feeling of alarm has fixated in a minuscule of jealousy that has now begun to creep into my loins. Even when Temple saw me with another woman in my lap, she didn't show any sign of jealousy or disdain. She hides her emotions well, allowing them to function through her daily routine.

No matter how badly I want to approach her now, I remain in the car for fifteen more minutes to allow her to get settled. Temple can't stand to be bothered as soon as she steps into her apartment. She may think I haven't noted anything about her, but I have.

And I appreciate all the small things that make her different from any of these other women I decide to entertain. Those small things have made me miss her.

The notion that she may not open the door for me lingers at the back of my mind. I take the chance to ring her doorbell. There has been no other way for me to contact her, and showing up tonight is my last resort. I can see the light change when she opens up the peephole.

"Temple, it's Aaron. Open up."

"Aaron, I have to work in the morning."

"Okay, I'm only going to take a few minutes of your time." The lie rolls off my tongue easily. If I have my way, I am going to be spending the night in her bed, delivering the type of makeup sex that always causes her to change her mind.

A few seconds pass before she swings the door open.

"Look, Aaron, you and I said all we needed to say outside the diner today."

She looks pissed off as she should. The first thing I plan to do is give her a massage. I see the glass of wine on the table beside the couch. Temple always curls up with a book before going to bed. I wonder why she isn't in bed until I notice the television on OWN. I know she is about to watch some sapped out, murder mystery with a twisted love story. As the wheels are churning in my head, she interrupts me.

"I really don't have all night."

"I understand. The boss has your putting in some long hours I see. We didn't finish our conversation today."

"Aaron, there was no real conversation. We decided that you and I were nothing. Now good night." From the glassy look of her eyes, I can tell she has already been sipping. And I can bet on that factor working well for me tonight.

"Babe, you are everything to me. I know I messed up. I just had a little too much to drink, and I let my boys get in my head."

While I am talking, I reach out to touch her shoulder cautiously, half expecting her to push my hand away. When she doesn't, I take a deep breath as I am one step closer to my goal to seduce her. Temple is allowing me to touch her, but she is still shaking her head back and forth while wearing a little smirk on her lips.

"So, you're going to blame it on the alcohol?"

I can tell she doesn't believe me.

"I need to blame it on something, babe. What else can make me go out of my right mind?" Temple has the answer. She is now looking at me with lust-filled eyes as I stand in front of her, kneading her shoulders.

"Why are you so tense, babe?"

The little sigh that comes from her mouth is all the encouragement I need to move right past the signs of caution by placing my hands under the nightshirt she is wearing. My wood instantly hardens with the thought of her not having on anything underneath the shirt. And then the fact that she is letting me touch her right now after my blatant disrespect gives me the rush to make my wood thump.

Whispering against her ear, how much I want her before leading her to her bedroom. The best part about this thing right here is believing that Temple has forgiven me once more. I swear I can't be held accountable for my philandering ways if she isn't taking care of business. And she hasn't let me touch her in weeks, swatting my hand away every time I have tried to touch her. Yeah, she must have found it in her heart to forgive me.

## Temple

Everything I am feeling right now, has got to be a result of all the pent-up desire and frustration from this last month. Knowing that Aaron has been constantly lying to me for at least that long, I haven't been allowing him to touch me. The expensively, delicious wine I'd had at the restaurant didn't require me to drink a lot of it to feel a buzz. Now tonight, I can blame these foreign feelings that kept creeping into my being on the alcohol.

The moment I sat down across from the man whose complete attire probably cost more than my whole salary for a month. His cologne serenaded my senses, playing a beautifully harmonious melody, the moment I sat down.. My throat had gone dry, and the moment he opened his mouth, I had to sip some water and wine before I could even remember the script I had written upon learning I would have dinner with him in Apryl's place. I'm not sure what turned me on more, the fact that he is out of my league; based on social status and wealth. Or maybe the wine awakened my hormones.

Whatever it was, I'm feeling it right now. Horny and buzzed. With a familiar mouthpiece in front of me , I decide to temporarily forget Aaron's blatant disrespect.

All the apologies in the world couldn't change the hurt caused by someone who is supposed to love and care about you. Yet they continuously disrespect you in such a way that other people look down on you. The girl who had sat on his lap the other night is now trolling me on social media as if I am the side chick. And apparently, he has made her feel that I'm no one of importance in his life. Just thinking about the whole fiasco causes me to lose some of my buzz.

Determined to get this feeling off, I close my eyes as I push Aaron's head down from my breasts to my nether region. Immediately, he sticks his tongue out and begins to lap and lave up the jism that has been pooling since dinner. Letting my head fall back against the pillows, I think of my first dinner meeting with Mr. Evans. From the moment I stepped out of my car and walked up to the restaurant, it was my very intention to blow him away. And when I saw him, I remembered him from the bar the night Aaron's side piece threw the drink in my face. The feeling of embarrassment tried to stifle my confidence. My throat instantly became dry, and I didn't think I could go through with this dinner.

The fact that Apryl and my friend Becca are depending on me propels me forward. Pushing every bit of embarrassment to the side, I picked up the glass of water to wet my parched throat.

After that, I proceeded to give Cairo Evans a little of our company's background then I commenced to sell Apryl's dream as if it were my own. I could tell that Cairo is impressed. But as quickly as I recognize that look in his eyes, it disappears. Just as I had witnessed him at conferences and meetings from afar, he upheld that "all about business" demeanor. Every now and then, he would nod his head while watching me over his steepled fingers. Thoughts of the pleasure he could bring to me with his hands alone invade my senses, bringing me to the way I am feeling right now, satiated with lust for a man way out of my league.

Aaron acts as if he is devouring his last meal. I admit it feels great. When he moans into my mound, it sends vibrations through me, and all I can imagine is it's Cairo Evans that I'm feeding. "Ummm, ssssss." I start sizzling.

When my hips rise from the bed, Aaron places both of his hands on either side of my thickness to keep me from pulling away.

"Don't run now." His warm breath tickles every sensitive nerve ending laying open and exposed. That orgasm that has been pent inside eases from me, causing me to push up on my elbows and dig my heels into the bed to push away from the cunning assault of Aaron's tongue.

"Where are you going, Temp?"

Hearing him call me by the nickname my father had given me causes anger to swell up in my stomach. Now it is as if he didn't just partake of me for my enjoyment. The orgasm has left me as I quickly remember how Aaron has violated our relationship yet again, and this time, he let me know that he has no regard for my feelings.

When Aaron smiles at me, I want to slap the smile from his face. Suddenly the need to get as far away from him as possible washes over me. I push myself from the bed.

"I need to use the bathroom."

"Okay, I will be ready for you when you get back." He is now getting out of his jeans, stroking himself like he is about to get a prize, I roll my eyes. Grabbing my cell phone from the dresser as I go the bathroom, I wish my brothers were near. Because I would call them to drag Aaron's sorry ass out of my apartment. But here I am thousands of miles away from my family, and I'm pretty much on my own. Tears sting my eyes, but I am determined not to let his sorry ass see me down. And I swear, my dad must have felt my heart, because my cell phone rings.

*Smoother than a gentle breeze*
*Flowin' through my mind with ease*
*Soft as can be, well*
*When you're lovin' me, when you're lovin' me, oh...*

*Sounds from my dad's favorite group singing one of his favorite songs, alerts me to his call.*

"Hey, baby girl. I miss you."

"Miss you too, daddy."

"How are you?"

"Apryl just sent me out with a potential client. I think my presentation of her vision may have gotten him to consider becoming her partner."

"It's good to hear that business is good. But I asked how *you* are doing?"

Sighing, I decide just to be honest with my father because I know he can tell something is wrong.

"I just broke up with Aaron."

"Good, I never liked that knucklehead anyway. He didn't hurt you, did he?"

Sighing, I decide against telling my dad the truth, although I am sure he has a feeling.

"No, he hurt himself."

"You don't need a man that doesn't value and respect all that you are, nor do you need a man that you can't respect and value either. Do you understand what I am saying to you, daughter?"

Facing my reflection in the mirror, I nod my head as if my father is looking back at me.

"I do, Daddy. I miss you so much."

"I miss you too, Temp. When are you coming home to see your family? Or do I need to make arrangements to come see you?"

"I'll be coming to see you soon."

"Alright. Call and check on your brothers, I overheard one of them telling the other they are having a new edition."

"A new edition to what?" This information changes my whole mood. News of one of my brothers finally having a child by their wives is exciting news for me.

"Call them and see," my dad chuckles into the phone.

"I love you, Daddy."

"Love you too, Temp. Good night."

After ending the call, I turn the shower on. Once I have cleansed myself, I slip into my floral cotton pajamas and return to my bedroom. Aaron has made himself comfortable by lying naked in my bed. The expression on his face tells me he is pleased with himself. It also tells me he needs to leave.

"Good night, Aaron."

He sits up to look at me with his eyebrows raised in confusion.

"Good night?"

"Yes, good night."

"I know you aren't going to just leave me hanging right now, Temp."

"Aaron, it's over. Good night." Although he continues to call me by my nickname, and it frazzles my nerves, I am determined not to become overly emotional. Nothing ever comes good when being led by emotion; I am very aware of this fact.

So, I chose to leave him on the bed, walk out of my bedroom, and stand at the front door of my apartment to wait for him. At least ten minutes pass before he meanders into the room with his boots in his hands.

"What's up with you, Temp-"

"My name is Temple. And I think you know what's up. I had a lapse of judgment by letting you in here tonight."

Suddenly, Aaron is pissed. He frowns at me as we stand at eye level.

"No, I get it; your ass was horny. I can't believe you used me like that. Is that what we have come to?"

Slowly, shaking my head at the audacity of him to act like he is hurt or bothered, I reply,

"I think you know the answer to that too."

We stand in silence for a few moments, before he finally reaches into his pockets to retrieve his car keys. He doesn't say a word as he stalks out my front door. Aaron doesn't even look back at me. Just the view of the back of his head as he leaves me is all I need to put in my mental Rolodex of him. It's over. Aaron and I can be no more. Pushing ill and hurtful thoughts of him out of my head, I secure the locks on my door, and grab my cell phone again. This time I send a text message to my brothers.

*Me: Alright, which one of you is making me an auntie?*

## Cairo

All night long, the woman who introduced herself as Temple has been running through my mind. Her slight smile, soft voice, and go get it attitude has made me consider Apryl Simmons' proposal to become her partner. Even though I had been dead set against even having this proposal presented to me less than a month ago when my assistant Stephanie brought it up to me.

The project to build a large enough property to house at least sixty impoverished families comfortably has a decent appeal. My father would most likely tell me to keep my hands out of it because there would be no great return in profit. Every time my sister is home with me, I am reminded that I can never forget where I came from.

Once upon a time, I lived with my mother, who could barely afford to pay for anything of luxury. If it wasn't a necessity, my mother would say I don't need it and nor will I get it. And I didn't get it until my father stepped in. He let me know I was born with a silver spoon. Now that I have the silver spoon in my hand my goal is to turn it to gold. Mr. Evans would argue with me. He would fight tooth and nail against me looking into this project. Now I am at my office waiting for Stephanie to arrive. When she finally makes it, she apologizes profusely for being late. And I remind her that I am the one who decided to come to the office an hour early.

"I plan to spend the afternoon with my sister, so I decided to come get some work done. Do you have any updates on Apryl Simmons and her project?"

"I'm sorry, I haven't been able to nail anything down with her. She is leaving town on Sunday and will not be back until Wednesday of this coming week."

"Did she leave someone in charge of things?'

"Yes, Temple-"

"I need her contact information as soon as possible." My request is a little too eager, causing Stephanie to look at me strangely. I clean up my request.

"I'd like to contact Ms. Simmons to let her know I am interested in learning more about her project. I'd like to implement a few of my ideas."

"Oh, okay. Would you like me to send them to her through email?"

"No, I need to sit down with her. You know I don't like sharing my ideas on paper." I had learned early that the people you least expect to steal from you will do it if given the opportunity. That's why I don't have any paper trails. Even though I don't consider myself to be in competition with anyone, there has always been someone out there competing with me.

"Right. I will get you that information, sir." The remainder of the morning, Stephanie moves a little slower than usual. I had expected that she would give me the contact information I had requested before I prepared to leave the office. Instead of giving me the information I had asked for, she sends me a bunch of crap that I don't care to look at all. So, I take it upon myself to pull up the agenda she had sent me a few days ago so I would know what to expect during the business dinner.

On the email, all Apryl Simmons information is easily accessible, and I am almost out with myself because I didn't think of the email sooner. It's not Temple's contact information. However, I am sure I can get what I need from Apryl. The moment I sit down in my car, I press

Apryl's contact information into the screen of my phone. Even though I am aware she is on her way out of town on business, I have business that needs to be handled. Another day going by without it will not do.

"Good afternoon, this is Apryl Simmons."

"Good afternoon, Ms. Simmons. This is Cairo Evans."

"Hello, Mr. Evans. To what do I owe the pleasure of your call?"

"I wanted to personally thank you for your invitation to partner with you on the housing project. I have a few ideas to run by you. I understand you are out of town on business this weekend."

"No worries, my assistant Temple will be able to give you all the information you need."

"Ah, yes Temple. Your assistant is very sharp and passionate about your brand."

"Temple is a great asset to my company. She is passionate about anything she puts her hands on. I couldn't ask for a better person to work with."

"Good to hear. I'd like to discuss this work soon."

"Ahh, yes. I need to touch bases with Temple to get her on board."

The need to reach out to her is so great, I decide to offer to contact Temple on my own-so I offer.

"I can get my assistant to reach out to Temple and we can go from there."

"Sounds good, Mr. Evans. I will send you her information." After ending the call, I feel a sense of relief because I am closer to my goal of reaching out to Temple. But unfortunately, Apryl Simmons doesn't make it a point to send the information right away. Not having control of this situation bothers me so much I am in a bad mood when I get home. Ivory detects it right away and calls me out on it.

"Why did you bring your work home with you?"

"What?"

"You're upset. I know it's nothing I did. So, I am assuming it is something that happened at work. Do you want to talk about it?"

Looking at my sister, I shake my head no.

"Come on, big bro. I'm not a baby anymore. You never know I may be able to offer you some sound advice. Especially if it's dealing with a female."

I'm sitting in my home office staring at the contact information for Apryl, trying to decide if I want to reach out to her again to get Temples info.

"I'm trying to decide how I want to approach this young woman."

Now Ivory looks very interested. She pulls her braids up into a bun as she sits down on the other side of my desk as if she is a client.

"What's stopping you?"

"She works for someone I am considering entering into a partnership with."

"Ohhh, okay. But what's stopping you?"

"She's different."

"Different how?" When I don't respond right away, she immediately begins to assume.

"I'm pretty sure you have chicks falling at your feet or knocking down your office door trying to get you to take them to bed. If you say she is different, I suppose she isn't one of them?"

Ivory's assumption is correct, so I nod my head.

"Let me ask you this. Why are you considering approaching her?"

"She's different."

"Okay, you have said that already. What interest you about someone who is different? She won't be some conquest or another notch to add to your belt, will she? Because if she is, I don't even know this chick, and I say you let her be."

"What? Just because she's different?"

"Nope, just because I heard you say you liked knocking women down and adding them to your wall of conquests."

Ivory smirks at me before telling me what she had overheard.

"Yeah, I suppose you thought I wasn't listening when you said that to one of your friends. If this woman is working and trying to build a name for herself, which it sounds like she might be, she doesn't need you getting in her way."

"How would I get in her way?"

"Big brother, you have it all right now, what would you want with someone who is climbing their way up a ladder to get what you have? If she's not a groupie and all you are interested in is getting her in your bed because she isn't fawning all over you, I suggest you leave her alone."

Finding myself not agreeing with Ivory, I decide to change the subject. I haven't thought much about why I want to approach Temple. When she came to dinner, she appeared to have it all together. Just listening to her talk business the way she had, surely piqued my interest. I'm the type of man who needs more than a grand entrance to get my attention.

But then I remember her from the bar as well. It had been messed up to see her walk in on her man having drinks with some random chick, then have that random chick throw a drink on her. Something about her that night made me want her. The thought crossed my mind that I would surely never see her again, yet she walked into the restaurant all about her boss' business to win me over. And she won me without a doubt. I wanted to know all the things she is passionate about. Yeah, this woman *is* different from all the rest of the women who have caught my attention. I guess it's true. I want her because she isn't trying to get my attention.

"Are you ready to go, Oprah?"

"Haaaa, jokes. Yes, let me grab my phone."

"Nah, no phones. It's just me and you today."

For a minute I think Ivory is going to fight me tooth and nail on that.

Yet I am surprised when she shrugs her shoulders before looking at me with a light in her eyes.

"No problem. The same goes for you." And I couldn't even argue with her. First, we went bowling. This had become one of our traditional past times. Every time Ivory comes home, we find a way to the bowling alley to spend time. While we bowl, I decide to strike up a conversation about her love life since she had tried to dig in mine.

"There isn't anything to tell."

"What do you mean? I know you have some knuckleheaded little boy sniffing at your dorm door."

When my statement makes her laugh, I know I have hit the nail on the head.

"I'm strictly focused on graduating at the top of my class next year. I don't have time to fraternize with little boys and girls." Her insistence is convincing. However, since she is blushing, I beg to differ.

Looking at my watch, "I find that hard to believe. So, you may as well go on tell me the truth. I have all afternoon and night."

"Urgggh! Come on, Ro. Let's bowl."

Now that she looks agitated, I back down for now.

"Let's bowl then." After bowling, we hit the cinema to catch the latest movie, then we head to her favorite Jamaican restaurant. My little sister orders a large bowl of plantains, curry goat, cabbage, and beans. The way she appreciates the meal makes me glad I decided to spend the afternoon with her. Looking up, I see a familiar face. Temple is standing with another female studying the menu. I may as well consider today my lucky day. I don't have to appear a stalker after all.

She is dressed in pair of white shorts that show of her long, brown legs. The plain navy blue t-shirt she is wearing hugs the side of her breasts nicely. Her hair is pulled back into a ponytail, making her appear a young girl. I am watching her giggle with the woman beside her, trying to decide how I am going to approach her. My sister taps her water glass with a spoon to get my attention.

"Hey, what's going on with you? Are you going to eat your food?"

When my food was brought out by the server, it was steaming hot. Now it sits in front of me lukewarm. And I still don't see myself digging into my meal before I say something to Temple.

"Yeah, I'm going to eat."

Ivory is a smart girl, so she follows my eyes to see what I am looking at. When something registers in her head, her face lights up.

"Oh, is that the girl that's different?"

There is no need to deny it, so I nod my head at my little sister.

"Have you decided how you are going to approach her?"

"Not really."

"Why don't you just say hello?" And I take my sister's advice before I lose the opportunity. Temple and the woman must have called in their food orders because they are already being handed their food. The chair makes a loud, scraping noise as I stand up from the table. Temple looks in my direction. As soon as she recognizes me, a slow smile spreads across her lips, then she looks away. Is that nervousness I see? If it is, then yes, she is different. I can't recall ever running into a woman who was nervous around me.

"Good evening, Temple."

Extending my hand to her with a smile, she looks at me with widened eyes, before placing her soft hand in my own.

"Mr. Evans, good evening."

Both women look at me with expecting expressions. Quickly, I clear my throat, deciding I must appear crazy right now just standing in front of them with nothing to say.

"I spoke with Apryl Simmons, expressing that I am hugely interested in learning more about the project. She stated she would be contacting you so we could sit down and talk about some details surrounding my coming aboard."

This must be news to her because she looks surprised for a moment. As she quickly recovers, she smiles at me.

"That is great to hear. It is a great project."

"Absolutely. Maybe we can discuss it over dinner soon."

"Dinner? Ah yes, dinner. Should I wait to hear from your assistant then?"

"Does she have your contact information?"

"I'm not quite sure, I know she has been in contact with Ms. Simmons."

"Allow me to shoot you an email."

"Okay, great. Temple@Simmonscorp.com."

Even though I am disappointed to be getting her business email, I nod my head reaching for my phone, then I remember that I had agreed to leave it behind.

"I agreed to leave my phone at home tonight while I spend quality time with my little sister. Do you mind texting your email address to me?" I explain while pulling a business card with all my info from my wallet. With relief that this may turn out to be a better plan than I thought, I reach for my wallet to retrieve a business card.

"No problem, I'll text you."

As soon as I return to my table, my sister gives me a thumbs-up as if I have just made some great chess move.

"Do you think she'll call you?"

"It's business-related, I hope so."

"I hope so too," she admits then returns her attention to the food left in front of her. "Please eat your food, bro."

Any other day, I would have devoured the meal the moment it was put on the table, but seeing Temple has me thinking of Infinite possibilities of getting to know more about her, and maybe devouring everything that is her.

## Temple

As we entered the restaurant, Becca looks at me with an incredulous expression. When I tell her about my encounter with Aaron, she quickly expresses her disdain for the whole situation.

"I can't believe you let his cheating behind in."

Becca rolls her eyes up toward the ceiling just before Cairo Evans approached me while we peruse the menu at my favorite restaurant. This place had quickly become one of my favorites, because they serve the finest Jamaican cuisine I have ever had. Although Beck and I had called our food orders in, I wanted to be sure there wasn't something I wanted to add to my takeout.

When I see Cairo Evans, I am surprised to say the least. This is a little mom and pop restaurant so I wouldn't expect someone with his status to step into. My mother had always told me never to jump to judgment when I meet someone. But all I have ever done is judge Cairo Evans, I have no problem admitting that.

My skepticism during our first meeting proved to be wrong as well. I expected someone who was stiff and uninterested. Yet, during the entire dinner, he showed genuine interest as well as an attitude that told me he is down to earth. Now that Becca is left looking after him with her tongue-wagging, I shake my head at her.

"Girl, forget Aaron's tired behind. That man right there looks as if he may very well be interested in you." She moves her head in the direction of the table Cairo is now sitting at. I hope he isn't looking after us, because if he is, I am sure he can tell that my friend is talking about him.

"Becca, nooo. The man only approached me talking about business." My face warms because for a fleeting moment that thought had crossed my mind.

"Okay, now how often does that happen on a Sunday, boo? Think about who that is, that is Cairo Evans."

"Becca, come on, let's be serious. This man couldn't be interested in anything except business. What do I have for someone like him? And I am surely not interested in a booty call after spending damn near two years in a relationship with a man who treated me as if that is all I am worth to him. Don't even get me started."

She sighs heavily as we step back out into the warm, balmy night. My friend feels like she is on to something and she just won't let it go.

"You know I really think Mr. Evans is trying to get to know you on a personal level. I mean, he has never showed an interest in working with someone, ever." Becca utters as we amble down the street toward my car. If I were naïve, I would believe in this fairy tale. Cairo Evans would come right in to sweep me off my feet, and we would both live happily ever after. But I never believed in fairy tales, even when my mother read them to me as a child. Even back then, a fairy tale just didn't seem possible for a girl like me. Playing off my feelings, I pose another question to Beck.

"How do you know? You act as if you know the man. You should quit with your theories, you know." Before she can even form the words to come back at me, who but Aaron steps out of a store with one of his close friends. Pausing my steps, I hope he doesn't see me, but of course, he sees me. Instead of continuing to go on about his business, I hear him tell his friend that he will catch up with him later. Becca sighs loudly,

"Temp, you know our food is going to get cold," she warns as we watch him walk in our direction.

"What's going on, Temple?"

"Hey." My dry response doesn't keep him from continuing to talk to me. After the other night, I thought he really got the picture. There is nothing left to say that will change my mind.

"Let's go somewhere so we can talk."

"Look, I didn't spend money on this food to just let it get cold. Besides, we don't have anything to talk about."

"I know you're not going to do me like that."

Becca rolls her eyes at him, "After the way you have been treating her? Man, please."

Aaron scowls, "So, Temple, you have been talking to your little raggedy ass friend about us?"

"Raggedy? Please. You would know about raggedy, wouldn't you?" She fires back at him. At this point, I decide to gently grab her arm and pull her along.

"Aaron, just quit while you are ahead, okay? It's over. I don't need a man that thinks it's okay to step out with other women whenever he feels like it." Just thinking about his betrayal makes me step a little faster, and now I feel I am dragging my friend behind me.

Aaron only pauses for a second with the unsure look of confusion, tainting the features of his face that I used to think were so damn sexy.

"I don't even know why I keep trying with you. You can't admit when you messed up; you act like you're some angel." This time, my mouth drops open as his words have created some shock value. Now his words have enraged me, and I want nothing more than to get my point across. Dropping Becca's hand, I turn completely around so that I am facing Aaron.

Becca knows I am about to go all the way in on him. Now she is pulling my arm trying to get me to continue walking toward my car, which is only a few feet away. Yet her tugging on my arm is useless.

"I messed up? Ha, I guess that lie that you continue to tell yourself is what makes you sleep well at night. But you know what? I'm going to let you keep that vision that, I, Temple, messed up our relationship. Now leave me the hell alone. I don't have anything for you." These words I yell at him, just as Cairo walks out of the restaurant.

Now she is urging me to come on. "Don't let this bastard get you out of character out here. You are about to make some major moves with Apryl and Cairo. Forget him," she whispers loudly. Aaron looks after us as I finally turn my back to walk away.

Now food is the last thing on my mind. We ride back to my apartment in silence. My mind is full of what if's. What if I had left Aaron the first time I suspected he had stepped outside of our relationship for sex? What if I had listened to my dad tell me over and over again that Aaron is no good for me?

"Are you alright? You know the only reason he comes at you like that because he knows he can upset you?"

"And it works every time."

"You know what though? You are going to take a deep breath, and when you exhale, you are going to exhale that negative energy. Now you have some business to handle."

Pulling up to my apartment, I notice a vehicle with out of state tags in the parking space that is designated as visitor parking for apartment A. When Becca visits, she parks her car in the extra spaces beyond my apartment.

"What's that, Becca?"

"Why don't you go ahead and text Mr. Evans your contact info, so you can get that meeting going?"

She hasn't noticed the vehicle I keep my eyes on as I grab my cold plate of food from the backseat. By the time I get out of the driver's seat, I scream as a man approaches me from behind.

"What you got there, girl?" No sooner than the surprise that caused me to scream leaves me, I whip around to hug my father. Tears spring to my eyes because I am so happy to feel his arms wrapped around me.

"Oh, Daddy! I missed you."

"I missed you too, baby girl. You know I can pick up on things like that." My mother and I are the shortest in the family. Only standing at 5'4 while my dad and brothers stand over us like giants at 6'1 and 6'2 and1/2.

"I hope you have something to eat in there because I can eat a horse." This comes from my oldest brother Tobias.

"You've been eating since you got on the plane, man. I'm sure you have already eaten a horse," my other brother, Trey, jokes with a smile. This sibling banter causes me to wipe my tears away with a smile. Memories of the days I spent listening to my brothers go back and forth. Feeling like there is no place I'd rather be. The only one missing is my mom.

"Where's mommy?"

"She had a conference to attend. Being that she would be out of town and wouldn't miss us, we decided to come see about you. Now, I would have to agree with Tobias, what have you got in there to fill my stomach?"

When Becca clears her throat quietly, I flush with embarrassment because I had forgotten my friend's presence just that quickly.

"I'm sorry you, guys. This is my friend Rebecca." Both my brothers look at each other with their eyebrows raised. No, my friend does not fit the description of someone who would be named Rebecca. She is used to the looks of surprise and confusion, so tonight, she smiles, "Hi, you must be Tobias, Trey, and Dad. You all can call me Becca."

Everyone looks at me strangely until I confirm that the shortage of her name is indeed okay.

"Becca and I just went out for some Jamaican food. Would you guys like to go out to get some? My food's gotten cold. What about yours, Becca?"

"I can heat mine up."

"Yeah, Jamaican cuisine sounds pretty good right about now. What do you say, Dad?" Trey adds.

"Whatever you guys want to grab, I'm with it."

"Come on, Becca. Let's ride."

"No, you go on catch up with your family. I have some work to do."

"You're always saying that when it comes to hanging out with my family."

"Maybe next time. I won't be good company tonight."

She gives me a hug before telling my brothers and father how nice it is to finally meet them.

"You don't have to leave, Becca We're good people; we don't bite or nothing," my brother, Trey, jokes, eliciting a smile from her.

"I know you're good people. I'll catch up with you all later. Temple, don't forget to send that contact information." She tosses over her shoulder as she makes her way toward her car.

"We didn't mean to run your company off."

"You didn't run her off, that's just how she is. It was like pulling teeth to get her to come out just to get the food."

"Sounds like the way you used to be."

My older brother observes with a smile. Deciding to put the food I have just bought in my refrigerator, I step inside of my apartment to do so. When my phone buzzes in my pocket, I remember to retrieve the card from Mr. Evans. Ignoring the text message alert from Becca, I compose a new message to Cairo, my business email, office telephone number, and my personal number. No matter what, he could reach me when and if he decides to.

## Stephanie

At some point in time, I have become a workaholic. Here it is a Saturday afternoon that I am choosing to work on a press release for Cairo instead of spending family time with my family. Every so often, I have caught my husband shaking his head at me while he plays with our kids. Even my mother gives me a few words of advice before she ventures off to a book club meeting. "Your family needs you too. You had better be careful before you lose what you have all because you are so focused on what you think you want."

I don't even bother to comment, because deep down, I know she's right.

Spread out in front of me are pictures that my colleague had taken of Cairo at dinner with Apryl Simmon's assistant. Jealousy creeps into my psyche as if it belongs. From the way Cairo seems to be looking at this Temple person as if she has intrigued him so much, I wonder what she has said to him so enthralling to have him ready to make commitments he had all but shunned before.

He has asked me about setting up another business meeting with her as if she is the one calling the shots. So many times I think I need to remind him that Apryl is the front runner. She is the one with the money and the title that will ultimately make things happen. As I look over each picture attempting to find the one with the best angle, my cell phone rings. When I see Cairo's name across the screen, I look around me to see if anyone is near me. When I am satisfied that I am alone, I pick up his call.

"Hello."

"Hello, Stephanie. How are you?"

"I'm fine. Is everything okay?"

"Everything is fine. I wanted to follow up with you on the information regarding Temple."

Inwardly, I sigh with aggravation because now Cairo has kept this woman's name on his tongue so often, I think I am going to start counting. Once I have collected myself by vowing to bite my tongue, I ask him what that information is. He tells me that he has gotten her contact information and would like to make contact with her within the next few days to discuss moving forward with the housing project.

The urge to ask him if he should make arrangements to have a meeting with Apryl herself and not her little assistant rises up in my throat like fresh bile. Clearing my throat, I swallow the urge, "Ms. Simmons reached out to me with said information as well. She will be back in town on Wednesday, sir, if you would like to schedule the meeting with her."

"I have another engagement that will send me out of town next week."

"Oh?"

This will be the first time I have heard of an engagement this weekend.

"My little sister and I will be traveling a bit."

"Okay, I am sure she will be available right after."

The next thing he says catches me completely off guard.

"Stephanie, I am beginning to think you are having trouble making sure this is done. I am aware Apryl Simmons is the leader of the project. However, in Ms.

Simmons' absence, she felt compelled to send Temple to represent her interest. And I feel that Temple has done a great job as Ms. Simmons expected. Now with that being said, I need to get this ball rolling quickly, did you not express to me there is a deadline of some sort that my company needs to meet in order to be considered in the list of fastest-growing Fortune 500 businesses?"

This simple question causes me to stammer my reply.

"Yes, there is a deadline."

"Isn't that deadline in a week?"

"Yes it is."

"Well, I want the name of my company on that list. Are you on board with making that happen?"

His question is an open challenge. Suddenly, I feel frustrated and embarrassed because being jealous had made me forget my role as Cairo Evans' assistant.

"I am on board, Mr. Evans. Have been on board since day one."

"Was worried about you."

"No worries. I will send you plans as soon as I pull them together tonight."

"Can I expect the plans within the hour?"

Looking at my watch, I inhale.

"Yes. I will get back to you within the hour." Suddenly, the bedroom door swings open and in walks my husband, Rodney, with a deep frown marring his most handsome features, his full lips, and his dark brown eyes.

"Are you going to come spend some time with us, Stephanie? We have been waiting on you since this morning. I can't believe that bastard has you up here working for his ass on the weekend."

"This is an outside project I have been working on. It has nothing to do with Cairo."

My husband allows a smile to creep across his full lips, which brightens his dark eyes just a bit.

"That's my girl, show that bastard you can make money moves without him." Now his envy is dancing with mine. Dropping my shamed eyes, I manage to come up with a quick answer.

"Give me an hour, honey. I will be right there. I love you." There is no missing the look of surprise that crosses

97

his face when I blow him a kiss. It has been a few weeks since I have taken the time to show my husband some affection. To let off some of my stresses, I decide this is something I need tonight.

## Temple

Sitting at a table at one of my favorite dinner spots with my favorite men feels wonderful. The issues with Aaron are far from my mind now. However, it seems to be the first thing on their mind. After my brother Trey wipes his mouth, he sits back then rubs his stomach.

"So, what's been going on, sis?"

Trey's question seems to be pointed. Before I can come up with a simple answer, Tobias chimes in, "We heard you broke up with that bum you thought was worthy enough to bring out here to California with you. Has he been giving you any problems?"

My big brother clasps his hands together while waiting for my response. There is no need to look at my father, because I know he is the ringleader. Determined to make sure no one messed over his baby girl, he decides to make his presence known.

"Y'all didn't need to come out here for that, I'm fine. Aaron isn't dumb."

Trey scoffs, "That dude is dumb as a ton of bricks, and you know it, sis. It's time you find a new man. Should

I get one of my homeboys to come out here to show you a good time?"

If my face could redden, it would be flushed in embarrassment. My cheeks warm and I begin to blush.

"Trey, really?"

"Sis, come on, let's be honest. This dumb dude has been wasting your time. You ignored all the good guys advances for his dumb ass. For that alone, he needs to be handled."

"Daddy? Really? What did you tell them?"

My dad chuckles to himself, "The only thing I told your brothers is that you broke up with that no good knuckleheaded boy."

"And we decided we were going to come out here to see about our little sis. Make sure you're good."

Unconvinced, I stare at my dad just a little while longer. Until he smiles at me and says,

"So, now that my belly is full, I'm ready to go lie down. How about we get out of here?"

My dad suggests while I continue to study him, trying to decipher whether or not he is telling me the whole truth. Trey and Tobias follow us out of the restaurant, and they allow me to drive the rental back to my apartment. When we arrive, it is still early, and my brothers don't seem to be affected by the time difference that much at all.

"Sis, where do you go to have some drinks?"

"Well, there is a little bar on the beach where me and Becca go from time to time. " As I describe the bar, it suddenly pops in my head that it may not be the best idea to take my brothers there because that is also where I'd caught Aaron and his side piece. However, I don't get the chance to suggest we go somewhere else.

"Let's go then."

Instead of debating, I freshen up, then change my shirt.

Fifteen minutes later, I am walking into the bar with my brothers; all eyes are on us. Some women give my brothers several once overs as if they are looking at meals. Others look at me with eyes blazing with envy. All I do is shake my head. Both of my brothers are married, and Tobias' wife is expecting their first child.

Since I am already dressed casually in a pair of dark wash, fitted jeans, and a bright yellow tube top, I don't need to change my clothes. Tobias strolls up to the bar like he owns the place while Trey walks through slowly, returning the lingering stares most of these females in here are giving him. Once we are all seated at the bar, the first female approaches. She's cute, but immediately I sense that she is catty from the way she rolls her eyes in my direction. My brother Trey misses it, but I keep my eyes on her.

Issuing a warning, "Trey, don't make me call Asia ."

When this female hears my warning, she looks at me like she has lost her mind, and I begin to laugh because I can feel myself getting worked up.

"Trey."

"Calm down, Temp. She knows not what she do." Tobias tosses back a shot of brown liquor without so much as a grimace.

Speaking my brother's name doesn't stop this chick from easing even closer to him.

She is so close I can smell her cheap perfume. It has been less than five minutes and the scent is starting to give me a headache.

"Hi, My name is Alexis." She bats her heavy lashes at my brother, who has yet to wave his hand in her face to show off his ring.

"What's up, Alexis? How are you doing tonight?"

"I'm doing fine now, handsome. Where are you from? I hear a little country twang."

"I'm from VA."

"Oh, okay. Virginia. I've heard of Virginia. That is across the map. What brings you out here? Are you looking for your queen?"

A coughing fit seizes my lungs, and I nearly drop the mixed drink the barmaid had just made for me. Little droplets of the drink gather at the corners of my mouth as I try my best not to laugh at this girl's corny ass line. Tobias pats my back, "Damn, are you alright?"

"Hell no." Patting my own chest, I cut my eyes at Trey.

"I came out here for my fam."

"Oh, that's nice. Do you want some company?"

"No. Honey, didn't you just hear him say he came out here for his family?"

This woman has the audacity to sneer at me while moving even closer to my brother. She is now tastelessly appearing to sniff at his ear.

"Bitch, no one asked you."

"Hold on. Now you're being just disrespectful."

My brother Tobias stands up on one side of me, while Trey and I look at this woman who calls herself Alexis.

"No, honey, she is being disrespectful and downright nosy. What do you want him that bad you have to step all over the next woman's toes just to get him?"

"Actually, his wife has already done that, Alexis. Check out the ring on his finger." Since my brother seems to be enjoying this moment, I decide to call him out.

"Where is she then?"

"I just told you, I came out here for my family."

Now with all three sets of eyes on her, she finally realizes how much we resemble each other. The look on

Alexis' face is priceless. Instead of saying anything, she rolls her eyes then stomps out of the bar.

Tobias chuckles, "Trey, I have told you to set these females straight from the moment they start batting their eyes at you."

"I wish you would." With exasperation, I cosign. Picking up my drink, which has become watered down, I sip it quickly to catch a little effect. As soon as I slurp up the remainder of the liquor, my brother orders me another.

"I don't think you understand that a man enjoys having women flirt with him some time just so he can turn them down."

"When were you going to turn her down, Trey? When she finally stuck her tongue in your ear?" I shake my head at him. As soon as the bartender places my drink in front of me, I don't hesitate to pick it up then sip.

"This dude should have stayed single," Tobias finally states while giving our brother Trey a pointed look that makes me raise my brows at him.

"Bro, don't start that. I hear enough of that at home."

Trey grumbles as he keeps his eyes on his drink.

"Oh, you do? Apparently, you don't hear it enough because your wife calls my wife so often to complain about all the numbers she keeps finding in your pockets, it's a damn shame."

When I hear this, I take the straw from my drink so that I can place the cup to my lips. I need to toss it back.

"Whoa, just what the hell have I missed?"

Trey begins to shake his head from side to side dismissively. In fact, he is now wearing a scowl. "I didn't come here to talk about my life. We came here to see what's going on with you, Temp. Dad is worried about you."

Now the tables have turned. Both my brothers are now looking at me strangely.

"What do you mean, he is worried about me? I'm fine."

"He doesn't seem to think you're fine. I mean, you came out here with that bum, and now you guys have broken up. You know mom and dad weren't fans of you coming out here alone to begin with."

Trey admits before he finally orders his drink. He appears to be glad he could change the topic of discussion. While I am not a fan of the new discussion one bit.

"I'm a grown woman; I think I am perfectly capable of handling myself out here without Aaron's ass." If my father really knew the details of Aaron and I, he would really be surprised. We have never lived together. With that being a fact alone, that should be enough to let my family know I am capable of handling myself just fine out here. The more and more I have thought about it, I think coming with me was just an excuse for Aaron to get away from his own family. In two years, he hasn't even tried to move in with me because moving in with me had its conditions. The number one of them being, I required a ring.

"But no matter what, you are still Daddy's little girl. Dad is having a tough time getting used to the fact that he can't protect you all the way out here. What do you think about coming home?"

Now both Tobias and Trey look at me expectedly.

"I'm really doing okay out here. The company I work for is on the brink of becoming one of the top leaders in housing. Apryl Simmons is also partnering with Housing mogul Cairo Evans."

As if I am a little girl again with something to prove, I spit out these big names to convince my brothers that my future is bright here. Suddenly, Tobias looks at me, "Cairo Evans?"

He speaks the name as if giving some type of recognition. So, I nod my head and repeat myself, "Yes, Cairo Evans." Then I realize my brother isn't looking at me. He is looking behind me. Slowly I turn around, and my heart drops to my feet. Cairo Evans is walking towards me. I don't realize exactly what's going on until my brother brushes past me with his hand extended toward Cairo.

"My man! Long time no see."

They give each other a handshake and a brotherly hug, leaving both me and my brother Trey looking on in puzzlement. I know who Cairo Evans is, but how does my brother know him well enough to be dapping him up and hugging him like a long-lost friend?

"It's been what damn near six years?"

"Something like that, congratulations. What are you doing down here with us little people?"

"Don't even do that, bro. I'm just like anybody else in here."

When Cairo finally looks at me, my brother apologizes for being rude.

"This is my baby sister Temple and my brother Trey."

Cairo shakes Trey's hand before looking down at me, speaking my name.

"Temple, small world."

When he extends his hand to me as if it is his first time meeting me, I blush while holding on a little longer than normal. My brother looks at Cairo for an explanation about what he meant.

"I met with Temple a few days ago, and she blew my mind with her presentation of a housing project. When my assistant brought it to my attention, it didn't catch my interest at all. But Temple put a spin on it that made me open my eyes to the possibility of it being a great project after all."

"Wow, this is a good dude, sis. Good dude." Tobias slaps Cairo's back just before asking him what he could order him to drink. Trey and I watch as Cairo and Tobias fall into conversation about who's who, where are they now, and so on.

"So, you know this dude?" Trey mumbles so low I barely hear his words.

"Well, I wouldn't say I know him. I know of him."

Trey studies me while sipping his drink. He has never been much of a drinker. Tobias and I have already ingested three shots. And I will admit, I am feeling fuzzy and tipsy. The warmth I am feeling has me openly checking for Cairo, and my brother Trey is taking note.

"How does Tobias know him?"

"I think they went to college together. I'm not sure, but I have heard Tobias mention this dude before. So, you work with him?"

"Not exactly. My boss has me trying to entice him to partner with her."

He nods while finishing his drink. "It seems like you have definitely enticed him to do just that." The way my brother slowly nods his head is as if he knows something he doesn't know. When I notice Cairo and my brother Tobias eyeballing me from the bar, I excuse myself to go to the restroom—fumbling for my phone along the way. I need to call Becca. Upon dialing my phone, I discover an itinerary for dinner the day after tomorrow with Cairo.

Suddenly my mind is taken over by thoughts of what I have in my closet to wear. When my friend answers the phone, the first thing I say is, "We have got to go shopping."

"Girl, it's almost midnight."

"I'm sorry. Can you meet me at the mall tomorrow?"

"Just come pick me up when you're ready to go, sheesh. Do you think I can go back to bed now?"

"Oh, Beck, you are so boring. It's entirely too early for you to be in bed."

Teasing my friend has become second nature. Becca is like the sister I never had but always wanted. Although she has two siblings, I have learned from our boss Apryl

Simmons that she has never been close to them as she is with me. In fact, her sister Stephanie stays in constant competition with her for a reason no one has been able to figure out. Even in the two years I have come to know Beck, she has never introduced me to her sister Stephanie, and sometimes I find myself wondering why that is.

## Cairo

During our conversation, Tobias had expressed concern about his sister.

"She plays that tough girl role, but she is so soft dudes take advantage of her. " He had complained with his sister only a few feet away from us. Temple's demureness is refreshing, while her approach to business is anything but unsure. During my first meeting with her, she made sure to garner my respect. She displayed a strong knowledge of the housing program, which made me want to listen. Whereas I had just got finished telling my assistant that I didn't want anything to do with Apryl Simmons' project or anything like it.

Aside from her attractive, doe shaped eyes, her soft-looking lips and, the soft curve of her hips. She tries to hide in those power suits. Right now, her round breasts are calling for my hands to reach out to caress them. Even during this short period of time that I have been in her presence, I have thought about rubbing my thumb across her hardened nipples, which are pushing against the yellow fabric of her tube top. Thoughts of hearing her moan when I place my lips against the exposed skin of her neck make me call for another shot of liquor to get my thoughts under control. I try to shake the thoughts from my head, but Tobias calls me out,

"I see the way you keep looking at my sister, dog."

This dude knows me well, so there is no need for me to try to deny it.

"She's an attractive woman. She caught my attention with her head."

When Tobias looks at me with his thick eyebrows furrowed, I immediately try to come up with better words. "Get your head out the gutter, my dude. Listen, I had dinner with your sister a couple of nights ago. It was impromptu; my assistant thought it would be a good look to have dinner with the woman the world is talking about right now. Apryl Simmons. Apryl couldn't make it, so she sent her assistant in her place. I am a firm believer she needs to make her a business partner."

Tobias looks confused, so I elaborate. "Your sister knows her stuff. This project, she knows it so well, I mean it is as if she came up with the blueprint herself.

You should be proud of your sister." Tobias crosses his arms against his chest as he cuts his eyes across the bar at his sister and brother.

"I am very proud of her for coming out here making the kind of moves that she has in the last two years. Hell yes, I am very proud of my sister. I just wish she could find a decent person to spend her life with. She deserves it."

The amount of ardor that he speaks of her makes me want her even more. I find myself cutting my eyes at her. While I'm looking at her, their brother Trey is looking at me. "I'm sure someone will come along and sweep your sister right off her feet. You seem to be worrying for nothing."

## Stephanie

After a night of serious romping in the bed while our kids slept all night, I ventured downstairs to cook my husband breakfast in bed. His feelings of neglect weren't unwarranted. I won't deny that I have been putting my work over my family on most days. The excuse has always been that I want to solidify my spot as Cairo's partner. He had been letting me handle so many of his affairs I feel like I'd be perfect for the position that he doesn't know he needs to fill just yet.

Especially on the horizon of this new urban housing project he has been thinking of. At first, he wouldn't consider it because he fills like his plate is full. I beg to differ; he can always make room for dessert. Now that I have pushed this project in his face, a little regret has been creeping up my spine like the chill that causes goose pimples to rise on my skin while watching a scary movie. Receiving the pictures of Cairo during dinner with Apryl's assistant has me wishing that I had pushed a different project.

Not a project that's loosely attached to a woman that has him looking like he found a new toy in the department store window. Ordinarily, none of the women Cairo has dated bother me. It was easy to see that he wanted them for one thing, although they stood with their shoulders relaxed as if they stand as debutantes at an annual ball. The prize indeed would be a taste of Cairo, but that is all it would be. A hot and heavy good night that would end as a soft kiss farewell in the morning. Nothing more. Not even a phone call. Cairo would be done and they'd get the picture quickly.

This woman Apryl Simmons sent in her place looks like she belongs in the picture with Cairo. And he is looking as if he is glad she is there. The need to put a stop to what hasn't happened yet suddenly behooves me. Now preparing a hearty breakfast for my husband is the last thing on my mind, but since I'd made up my mind that I would fix him a big omelet and pancakes, that is what I intend to do.

Soon after placing the dish in front of him, I decide I need to present some kind of diversion. This woman who

Apryl sent to represent her has piqued Cairo's interest. His body language says it all, because he is good at keeping a poker face. I have come to know this man well enough to know he sees something in this woman. Even I see that she is different. She isn't flashy, begging for attention. She isn't overly aggressive Although I have decided there is nothing special about this girl,
my womanly intuition tells me that Cairo sees something special about this girl.

    His body language tells me he wants her when I need him to be focused on me. The photos that I suggested being taken were supposed to be for publicity, and there had been no bad pictures taken at all. Each photo captured passion and intrigue. There is no way for someone who studies facial expressions, and body language can miss the way he looks at her.

    "Baby, I need to run to pick up something from the store." Looking at my husband with a slight smile, hoping he won't question me too much.

    "What happened to you sleeping in?"

"In your famous words, I'll sleep when I die." My husband looks after me as I make my way the bathroom to take a quick shower. A plan is forming in my mind of how I can stop anything from happening between Cairo and Apryl's assistant. The warm water feels good against my skin. I close my eyes for a second when a swift breeze whips into the shower, my body tenses. Looking through the foggy glass of the shower, I see the silhouette of my husband standing naked. A protest catches in my throat as he steps into the shower with me. He is holding my pink loofah in one hand, and a bottle of my favorite body wash in the other.

"Let me wash your back." His deep voice echoes between the walls of the shower and the glass door. Deciding to swallow my protest, I sigh quietly, as my plan to throw a monkey wrench in Cairo's impromptu business dinner, skitter out the window. This man of mine is doing everything he can not to let me out of his sight. I know him very well, and in order to avoid an unnecessary argument, I relax my shoulders and allow him to work the loofah across my wet back.

As the frothy white suds slide down my spine to the crack of my buttocks, my nipples tighten. A yearning sensation begins to spread from the pit of my stomach to the surface of my vagina. I anticipate allowing his fingers to caress everywhere that the loofah has touched. When he does this, another sigh slips from my lips, and I place my palms against the shower wall to hold my body steady.

Slowly, I close my eyes and allow my head to fall back against his shoulder. The whole while, he uses his strong fingers to push my thighs apart so he can stroke me. Each stroke sends me closer to that ecstasy he introduces me to so effortlessly. As soon as guilt creeps into my psyche, I close my eyes tighter then commence to pushing that trip away. Why should I feel guilty for having feelings out of my control? After all, I have always loved Rodney with all my heart; things changed when I discovered the depth of his betrayal.

*Flashback*

*His betrayal began with a woman and ended with that woman carrying his child for nine months. I didn't find about the child until he received a call at two in the morning. When he got out of our bed, holding his cell phone at his ear, I didn't move from my comfortable position. He had been holding me in his arms, and it feels good. In his line of business, phone calls at two in the morning aren't uncommon. What made me sit up and take notice is the way he started talking in hushed tones, telling whoever to calm down. Ten minutes pass before he gets out of the bathroom, then he immediately begins throwing on his clothes. Again, isn't unusual for my husband. He's a bondsman, so he's always ready to go for the right price. Rodney didn't even look in my direction as he grabs his keys from the dresser. Normally, he tells me what he's about to do next, but when he says nothing, red flags go up all around my head.*

"*Are you okay?*"

"*Yeah-yeah,*" *he began with a stutter.* "*Man, I'm not sure if I can help this dude.*"

"*Oh? What's the charge?*"

"*Assault with a deadly weapon, possible murder one if the other dude doesn't live.*" *By this time, I am seated at* the side of the bed. With the warmth of his body absent, I no longer want to lie alone. "Is there anything I can do to help?" Although my question comes from a genuine place, he frowns at me as if I have asked something wrong.

"What do you mean, is there something you can help me with? It's two o'clock in the morning; I don't even want to be going out here right now."

"But you are, and you always do. And if I'm up, I always ask you if there is something I can help you with. What's different this time?"

Rodney rolls his eyes dramatically. "Don't start this shit, Stephanie. I'm not in the mood for it."

Rodney doesn't say anything else before he walks out of our bedroom. My cheeks are flaming hot from embarrassment. I can feel the tears begin to burn the back of my eyes as all the different scenarios begin to pop in my mind. There is something fishy about this call, and I am unwilling to believe it had come from someone who had been arrested on assault with a deadly weapon charges. Feeling extremely suspicious, I grab my jogging *pants from the chair, and I rush outside to my car with a plan to follow my husband, but when I make it outside, he has already backed out of the garage. Desperation takes over me. I call up my cousin in law enforcement to find out if he will tail him. My cousin normally works the early hours of the morning. Of course, he isn't happy about my request, but he is my family. Just off that notion alone is enough to get him to do this harmless thing for me.*

*A few hours later, he called me with news that would change my life forever. I can remember the phone call clearer that day. "Are you sure you want to know what your husband is up to?" The apologetic tone of my cousin's voice caused my heart to still momentarily.*

*As soon as my heart began to beat again, I closed my eyes then breathed my response. "Yes, I do."*

*As I waited for my cousin to speak words that would scorn my very soul, my phone vibrated in my hand. I had received a text message from my cousin. "I'm sorry, cousin. Let me know if I can do anything for you."*

*Tears clouded my eyes as I downloaded the video of my cousin following my husband to the hospital where he visited the nursery. A clear bassinet faces the window, giving me the view of a little brown baby wrapped snuggly in a blue blanket. My cousin zeroed in on the name on the basket.*

*Baby Williams. Mother V. Collins: room 203.*

*That day was the day I could only find refuge from reality inside my mind, and even there, I became a prisoner.*

*Needing someone to talk to, I called my boss Cairo Evans. He should be the last person I confide in. But I needed someone to listen or I would go crazy as hell. Cairo listened, although he was going through a battle himself. I could see the turbulence in his eyes.*

## Cairo

The next day my little sister knocked on my bedroom door. "Yeah," I call out as I'm sitting at my desk looking over work emails. When she jingles her keys, I glance at my watch.

"Come on, big bro."

"Come on, big bro? Do you know what time it is?"

"It's nine a.m., and if you can sit in front of your computer at this time of morning, on a Saturday morning at that, then you can surely get up to hang out with your little sister."

When she bats her pretty eyes at me, I laugh, wondering if that is what our mother had done to get my dad in her bed. "You're right, let's go."

After slipping on a pair of sneakers I slid into the passenger seat of the truck I gifted her for all her hard work. As we pull out of my neighborhood, my sister is quiet as she maneuvers the vehicle with ease through the city streets. Surprisingly, she doesn't have any hip hop floating through the speakers. She doesn't even have the radio on. It isn't until she has driven several miles down the road and pulled up to a stoplight, when my sister finally says, "So, are you having any thoughts about the meeting you are due to have with that young lady tomorrow?"

"Honestly, no." Of course I'm not telling the whole truth. Temple has been on my mind. Her brother, Tobias, has made an even greater case for me to pursue her.

But I decide to keep my thoughts to myself. I'm not sure if I will. The last time I tried to have a normal relationship with a woman, it didn't end well. She couldn't keep my attention at all because all she had to offer me was her body. In my early twenties, I could deal with that. Now that I am approaching my thirties, I desire more. And up until I rubbed elbows with Temple, I was good with being alone. Despite the stories my sister has to tell about my philandering ways.

"I think it is a great thing that you are interested in someone for more than sex. I applaud you, big brother. It's about time you settle down. But you know what would be even better?"

Suddenly I have the feeling that my kid sister is about to say something I don't agree with. Inhaling, I look out the window at the scenery around us. The tall, long leaf pines and the pleasant fields of green weeds are gently blowing with the breeze on this peaceful Saturday morning.

"It would be even better if you and I went to see our mother and you finally forgive her."

The feeling of peace leaves me rapidly. I'm suffocating now in the reality that I have not said more than a few words to my mother in three years. Ever since, I had to take Ivory in because my mother had offered my sister's virginity up to a drug dealer just so she could have a fix. The state my mother had been in I had never seen. It was like something I had read in a Shannon Holmes novel. My mother was strung out on the worst drug- heroin. Her once beautiful, olive tone skin had ugly purple splotches, and track marks ran up and down her arms like little tattoos, which symbolized the beginning of death.

She binged on drugs and alcohol for a whole year after I took custody of my sister. Then one day out of the blue, my mother called me begging to be saved from herself. The price to have her committed to one of the best drug rehab facilities in the country had been steep. But I paid it because I love my mom and I needed to see her healthy again. She spent eight months in rehab. As soon as she got out, I bought her a house. All her bills are automatically drafted from my bank account, all the way down to her grocery bill.

My sister is now looking at me with tears shining in her brown eyes. I can feel her expectancy, and it weighs greatly on me. Even though she hasn't said enough to tell me just how much she expects from me.

"Before you say you won't, Ro, our mother is very sick. She won't live too much longer."

Minutes pass, and I don't speak, I don't even think I am breathing. But I'm suffocating. I've been suffocating since my sister began speaking of our mother. Now my kid sister is suffocating too.

For the last three years, I have done everything I know how to do to protect her. Still somehow, my mother has managed to pull my sister into her turmoil.

"The light is green." I don't know what else to say now. Tension has now become so thick in the car, I tell her to pull over so I can get out. Ivory pulls into an empty parking lot. Then she watches me as I open the door. My world has now become unsteady. With my sister away at school studying, my business has been running just the way I need it to- my life seems under control. The last thing I need is something to throw everything I have worked hard to maintain to be thrown off balance.

"Cairo, did you hear me? Please say something," Ivory says as she gets out of the car to stand with me. But I don't want her beside me. I want to shout for her to get back inside until I figure out how to regain control of everything that seems to be spinning out of control. I know she doesn't understand. She doesn't deserve to feel the effects of my uncertainty.

"How do you know, Ivory?" These are the only words I can muster.

Ivory is quiet for a few minutes. When she finally turns to face me, tears are running down both her cheeks.

"I talk to her every day, Ro."

"How do you know she is telling the truth? Do you remember all that happened three years ago? Surely you couldn't have forgotten."

"I went to see her, Ro."

"How did you go see her when you have been in school?"

Ivory drops her head, leaving me to suspect that the next thing she says will be something else I don't care to hear. Birds are chirping happily in the distance as the flow of traffic continues around us.

"Answer me, Ivory." I look directly into my sister's eyes, silently daring her to look away.

Finally, she admits, "I caught a ride on the weekend to go see her."

"You weren't supposed to leave campus. What if something had happened to you?"

"Nothing did, Ro."

"But what if it had? Don't you understand how much more stress that would have caused in my life? I tried to protect you from her, Ivory. Now you are standing here telling me you have been catching rides to the city to see her while lying to me, telling me that you have been in school? What else have you been lying to me about, Ivory?"

"Nothing and I didn't lie."

"When I called to check on you on the weekends, what would you tell me? Huh?"

Ivory doesn't realize the betrayal until now.

"I'm sorry, but she needed me." She looks around helpless, nervously rubbing her hands together.

"Just like she needed you when she tried to sell you to pay for her drug habit right?" Now I can't help it, I am raising my voice at her, and she is crying softly now.

"She was sick then too. But you made sure she got better, Ro. You did everything you could do her son and as my brother. Thank you for everything you have done for our mother. This time you can't fix it, Ro."

The weight of her words are unexpected. All my life, I have been able to fix anything that has posed as an obstacle. I am unwilling to accept what Ivory has said to me. My heart starts feeling heavy, and I clutch my chest as it begins to feel tight. I haven't felt this way in a long time.

When I begin to walk away from the truck, I hear Ivory calling after me.

"Ro, I'm sorry. I'm sorry. Please don't leave me too." When she says *too,* my heartbeat slows down. And I turn back around to face her.

"I'll never leave you, Ivory. But you have got to understand what I am trying to do. I am trying to protect you."

"I'm sorry, Ro. But she's dying."

Pulling my sister into my arms, I give her a strong hug. Even though I know it won't ease the pain she feels knowing that she is going to lose the one person she thought would always be there.

Shedding tears is foreign to me, so when I feel the wetness beneath my eyes, I immediately wipe it away.

And I tell my sister that everything is going to be okay. Even though I haven't spoken more than ten or fifteen words to my mother in the last several months, I am willing to do what I can to make what may be her last days more comfortable. Deep down in my heart, I am unwilling to accept that she has been given a death sentence.

"Let's go see about her."

Ivory looks at me with uncertainty clouding her eyes.

"Are you sure?" Nodding my head is all I can do in response because I'm not sure of too many things right now. My world isn't turning the way it has always done. Thirty minutes later, my sister is pulling into the parking lot of my mom's home.

I bought my mother a house in a small neighborhood just outside the city. This neighborhood is safely tucked away from all the temptation a recovering drug addict could find in the middle of our city. No crack fiends on the corner. No pimps looking for their next piece of ass to put a price on. No drug dealers pushing anything to anyone willing to poison their bodies with the lethal shit that made them hood rich. No, I paid a hefty price to make sure my mother wasn't exposed to any of that.

Instead of seeing crack fiends walking the neighborhood at all times of the night and early morning, she would see middle-aged to elderly couples walking their dogs, jogging to get some exercise, and just maybe you might see someone's grandkid selling lemonade from their homemade stand.

I couldn't help anything that she had been through, but I could do everything possible to make sure bad things wouldn't continue. I love my mother with all my heart, but the last straw for me was having to rescue my little sister from the clutch of a treacherous drug dealer.

His demise would be something that I would take to my grave, and now it looked as if I would be taking my mother to hers. When we arrived at her home, she hadn't been expecting company. But my sister called her to let her know we had arrived. It hurt me to my soul to see a shell of the woman I called mommy. Even when she was strung out, she kept herself presentable. One could never tell she was a crack fiend. Her hair had always been immaculately laid by the best hairdresser money could buy. Even her clothing would throw you off. My mother didn't look like a coke head, crack head, dope fiend at all. She hid her addiction well.

Today, however, the woman I have always known to be fly, looks like death. Her 175-pound curvaceous frame is now about 95 pounds soaking wet. Her hair dull and gray has been pulled back into a ponytail that doesn't suit her at all. Her once bright, honey brown skin is dull and sagging everywhere that used to be tight. The housecoat she is wearing hangs from her body like a heavy cloak that can shield her body from rain.

"Ro, you came. My sweetheart, Ivory, you got him to come. Thank you, baby." My mother walks over to where I am standing in the middle of her living room. When she pulls me into her embrace, what is inevitable for me happens. Simple words betray my lips and I can't express myself. All I can do is weep like the ten-year-old little boy that always cried on his mother's shoulder. She would always find a way to comfort me with her words. "It's going to be alright, Ro." Although my mother is saying these words to me right now, I know better. This time it won't be alright.

"How can I fix this?"

"Baby, you can't fix this. I have to pay for my sins."

"Mommy, this is no way to pay for your sins. You have lost a lot already. You shouldn't have to lose your life." I'm not even embarrassed because I sound like a spoiled kid right now. Here I am standing 6'1 and a half over my mother's 5' 4 frame. She takes me by the hand, then leads me to her couch. Just like an obedient child and not a grown ass man who has everything all figured out, I sit on the floor at her feet.

"Baby, I have waited and waited for the day when you would come to me. I have apologized over and over for everything I have done wrong to your sister, and I have prayed that she would forgive me. The one thing that I could never grasp is that my son, my baby boy, wouldn't forgive me. I'm sorry. The drugs had my mind a mess."

Feeling the need to stop her from talking or my heart might just explode, and it will leave my sister with nobody. I grasp her hand in mine.

"I love you, mom."

"I love you too, son. I love you too."

After several hours of just soaking up her presence, I excuse myself to call my assistant Stephanie. When she answers my call after the first ring, it is as if she has been waiting by the phone for a call. "Cairo, it's late. Is everything okay?"

Stephanie knows I never call her with anything after eight p.m. The clock reads nine thirty five.

"I want you to postpone the dinner with Temple tomorrow."

"Postpone dinner with who?"

"Temple, she is Apryl Simmons' assistant."

"Oh, oh yeah right. You want to reschedule dinner?"

"Postpone it. Let her know I will reach out to her as soon as I can. Something urgent has come up." Looking at my sister sitting on the couch with our mother is all I need to see to make me decide to put everything in my life on hold. Nothing is more important than these two women.

"Oh, okay. Can I help you with anything at all? Is your little sister okay?"

"Thank you for your concern, Stephanie. I really appreciate it. Contact Temple for me and I will be in touch soon."

The line is silent for several seconds before she finally agrees. "Let me know if you need anything at all. What about your meetings abroad starting Monday?"

"Postpone everything if you will."

"I will take care of everything."

"Thanks." Hanging up the phone, I don't give her a chance to ask me if I need anything else. At this point, there is nothing in this world anyone could ever do for me. My world must stand still so that I can bury my mother.

## Six Months Later...
## Temple

Becca and I are seated with the rest of the Simmons Group staff waiting for Apryl Simmons to step on the stage to accept the award for this year's top businesswoman of the year. She is also being recognized for her amazing work on the housing project with Cairo Evans. In just a few short months, over fifty-two families will finally be able to move into a place they can call home.

We made it a point to focus on families who had lost great amounts in the most recent national disasters that have impacted our communities even more so the impoverished who have been overlooked maybe not intentionally yet still, forgotten.

Apryl admits it wouldn't have been possible without the tireless efforts of Cairo Evans and their staff. When Becca and I hear Apryl call our names and even ask us to come to the stage to be recognized, my heart drops to my feet. But I make sure no one can tell how nervous I am. This award show is being televised as we speak, and hundreds of people are in the audience applauding. In fact, by the time we reach the stage, the audience is now standing to their feet giving us a standing ovation. Somehow, I end up standing beside Cairo. The man is so damn handsome in his grey pinstriped suit, which again just as I had concluded many months ago, he had perfectly tailored to fit his sexy body. Even though I hadn't seen him since our impromptu meeting at the bar, the night my family showed up at my door, I hadn't forgotten the obvious energy between us each time we have had an encounter. The night I learned Cairo and my oldest brother Tobias are frat brothers for life had surprised me. My brother has never mentioned any of his frat brothers, yet he had seemed so fond of Cairo. I admit I had been a little more amazed than anything.

As I'm lost in my thoughts, I feel a gentle touch at the small of my back. I almost leapt off the stage. If Becca hadn't been holding my hand, I probably would have. Cairo is touching me. Again, I am surprised, but I don't move.

"I meant what I said when I said, I know I wouldn't be as successful if I didn't have these two brilliant ladies on my team. And I want to thank you. You deserve just as much recognition as I do because we have been in this together from the very beginning, Becca, thank you. And Temple, my goodness, you opened my eyes so much. You helped me put it all together, thank you. This award belongs to you just as much as it does to me. I wouldn't be here if it hadn't been for you ladies. I know it. Thank you. Thank you. Thank you."

Again, the audience applauds loudly, and someone comes to lead us off the stage. Never have I been so happy that I took the chance by leaving home. Just the thought of how far I have come makes my eyes mist.

"Temple." A deep, familiar voice pulls me from my moment of reflection. When I look up, I look into Cairo's deep, hazel eyes.

"Mr. Evans."

I suppose the formal way I greet him causes him some surprise because he pauses before saying, "Please, call me Cairo. I want to thank you for your tireless work over the last few months. Even in my absence, I will say I noticed your dedication to this project. Thank you."

"You're welcome. This project was something I really believed in, and I am so glad you changed your mind about getting involved."

Cairo drops his eyes from mine for just a second. "I'm glad I changed my mind too."

Becca, who had been just a few steps behind me, comes up to where we are standing. She pulls me into her arms for a hug, obviously not taking notice of the man talking to me.

"Girl! Talk about out work paying off! Did you know she has given us an all-expense paid vacation to Jamaica?" My coworker turned best friend, more like a sister, smiles brightly. In fact, I can feel the excitement radiating from her. Hugging her back, I whisper wow with surprise. It is then that she notices Cairo standing close to me.

"Oh my, forgive me."

"No need to apologize. You both deserve it for all of your hard work."

"Yes, I'm going to grab a drink. Temp, call me before you leave." Becca hugs me once more before leaving Cairo and I alone again.

"You're probably wondering why I'm in your personal space. Now that we can rest a few minutes I wanted to invite you to dinner."

I feel the need to swallow hard before responding to his shocking request.

"Dinner? I, uhh-"

"No talking about business, I just wanted to get to know a little more about Temple. You intrigued me so much. After all the craziness that came with the hard work we had to put in to complete the project, all I could think about was the woman who presented this project to me and the way she presented it to me."

How he speaks of me causes me to blush inwardly. Feelings of warmth flush my cheeks, and my stomach flutters. "Okay."

"Sounds good. Now this is going to sound way off the wall and I respect your response if you say hell no."

All I can do is raise my eyebrows at him because I can't imagine anything he could say off the wall. But what he says next is truly surprising and weird, to say the least. As if he knows I can't yet comprehend his question, he repeats himself.

"Apryl and I discussed sending you guys on an all-expense paid trip to Jamaica. Of course, we are going to take a break too, and I wanted you to accompany me."

"Excuse me? You mean, you are asking me to go with you to Jamaica after just having dinner once? What if I'm some undercover, crazy, deranged person that is using this calm, composed demeanor as a front because I plan to rob you blind?" Even how quickly I come up with the scenario surprises me. But all Cairo does is smile.

"I doubt that very seriously, I know your brother."

"What if you are the undercover, crazy, and deranged person?"

This didn't appear to be something he had thought about. "I understand if you say no."

I could hear my friend telling me I should learn to live a little. I could also hear her telling me that I am crazy for even thinking negatively about his invite. The last several months I have put my all into my work. My only means of socializing has been with Becca and my family. Every so often, I would have fleeting thoughts of the companionship of the opposite sex. For the most part, I have put my energy into my work and getting in tune with myself. After a short debate, I finally agree.

"Okay, when would you like to go?"

"I'd like to leave Sunday."

"Sunday? You know that is the day after tomorrow."

"Yes, I know it's short notice. You can bring your friend along."

Before I can say another word, a young girl probably about sixteen or seventeen years old appears, calling out to Cairo. "Wow! I really feel like a celebrity." She appears to be the typical teenager.

"Ivory, stop acting like I don't take you anywhere." She looks at him with widened eyes just as she swats his arm. "This is my kid sister, Ivory. Ivory, this is Temple."

Ivory whips her head around just slightly to look at me. "Temple!! Wow, finally! Mommy would be so proud."

Cairo shakes his head as if he is a tad embarrassed while Ivory holds her hand out to me, "I'm glad to finally meet you, Temple. When my brother told me a little bit about you the night you and your friend was at the Jamaican restaurant, I'd always wanted to meet you."

"Nice to meet you, Ivory."

I'm not sure what more to say at this point. In fact, I can't believe I have just agreed to be a guest on a vacation with a dude I don't really know. But as the saying goes, you only live once.

## Stephanie

After watching Cairo, Apryl Simmons, Temple and my sister accept an award for their hard work, I turn the television off with a huff. My husband, Rodney and I had been watching the show together. I was okay until Apryl Simmons gave her crew credit, but Cairo kept his mouth shut about the team behind him. He didn't do anything on his own, yet he didn't even invite me to the show. I'm sitting on my living room couch watching it like a distant fan.

"Oh hell no! Stephanie, you need to quit. After all the work you have been putting in in the name of Cairo Evans, you didn't even get invited or mentioned tonight? That is absolute bullshit, and you know it. That man owes you half of everything he's solely taking credit for. Even your sister was getting recognition on stage!!" His criticism isn't making the feeling of betrayal better at all. I am so enraged I grab my phone to text my sister, Rebecca.

Before I even press send, my husband says something that enhances the enragement that I already feel. "It seems like you should be working with your sister. At least the woman she works for has more loyalty than the dude you work for." I don't know what bothers me the most, about his comment.

When I feel myself start trembling and my breath quiver, I press end on the phone. Although I can hear that my sister has picked up my call. The way I scoff scares me, and I believe it scares him too because he stops laughing to look at me with widened eyes.

"Now, I don't think you can talk about loyalty at all when you have a three-year-old son running around here that I didn't birth. No, I don't think you would be the one to talk about someone's lack of loyalty."

Rodney becomes quiet as he studies me. "That was a mistake."

"A mistake is oops I picked up the wrong cereal at the supermarket. An oops, is taking the wrong exit on the interstate because you thought it looked like the one you took the last time. A mistake isn't that little boy running around with your last name, Rodney. Just know before you go bashing someone about loyalty, you don't have any room to talk."

The next thing that comes out of his mouth punches me so hard in the gut, I almost double over in pain.

"Yeah, well, the woman who birthed that little boy who is running around here with my last name never made me question who the hell she is loyal to."

"So, are you saying you cheated because you questioned my loyalty? Is that what you're saying to me right now, Rodney? If that's what you're saying to me, then I don't even know why you stayed here. Go be with that woman. She deserves all the love and loyalty you can give her."

In a huff, I leave my husband standing in the living room looking after me. I rush down the hall to our bedroom so that I can grab my car keys and purse. After collecting these things, I turn around and end up running right into my husband's chest. When he tries to wrap me in his arms, I violently push him away, causing him to stumble against the door of our bedroom. You can hear the harsh sound of plaster splintering. I am sure when the doorknob crashed against the wall, it had made a hole. But I don't even stop to survey the damage.

"Get off me."

Luckily, our children are in bed, and I don't need to worry about them asking where I am going.

"You took it wrong, calm down."

"Ha, how else was I supposed to take that?"

"You're overreacting. All I said is that you need to find another job, one that recognizes your hard work."

Stopping at the door, I look at my handsome husband from head to toe. When I met him, I had qualms about getting to know him beyond friendly hellos. I had learned from my mother, and almost all the women in my life, that it is better to be cautious with your love because if you love with your entire heart, and that man knows it, he will surely send a dagger right through it and then act like he hadn't done a thing.

"Steph, what the hell is it going to take for you to love me?"

"Loving you hasn't been easy, you know?" These words still him. He looks at me as if he is looking into the eyes of a perfect stranger for the first time. Something tells me that the relationship we had been trying so hard to keep together for the sake of our children is now over.

The way Rodney stands looking at me from the doorway as I get in my minivan makes me wish things weren't going to end this way.

At first, I don't know where I'm headed. The need to get away had been overwhelming, so I ran. It isn't until I receive a text from my sister that I decide to pull up to her apartment. Maybe she would finally agree with me that I need to leave Rodney's ass once and for all to give the man who is most deserving of my love, loyalty, and patience.

My sister opens the door for me with the look of amusement on her face. At first, I think she's amused because I'd come to visit her at this time of night. But I quickly discover, she is amused with something her friend had said. Rebecca has her iPad propped up by a stand facing her. The person she is on facetime with is going on and on about not having anything to wear in her closet.

"Temple, you should be ashamed of yourself. I can find a whole new wardrobe with tags in your closet." When I hear exactly who she is talking to, my shoulders drop.

"Well, you should come over to find something to wear."

Before she gives me her complete attention, she sighs. "I'll call you back, Temp." As soon as her friend disappears from the screen, Rebecca looks at me.

"Tell me, what do I owe the pleasure of your lovely visit this evening." The slight tinge of sarcasm is evident in her voice, and I feel guilty for coming to burden her with my problems. But I need to talk to someone. After all, her friend may end up being a problem for me. The pictures that I had never given to the magazine that my good friend had taken of the two of them are still in a drawer in my desk. Every so often I couldn't fight the urge to look at them. At first, I thought he was the only one who had interest in his eyes, but I was wrong. Little Miss Temple has the nerve to have the look of interest in her eyes too.

"Hello, Stephanie. Did you come here to daydream? What's going on?"

"I'm thinking about leaving Rodney. His betrayal has become a little too much for me to deal with. I don't think I can take it anymore."

My sister rolls her eyes toward the ceiling. This is when I know she isn't happy about my visit. Although I have come hoping she would side with me and make me believe what I keep telling myself, I know I need to pull it together before I don't get the chance to plant the seed I didn't know I had intended to plant until I saw her friend.

"So, what makes you believe you are ready to leave this time?" This isn't the first time I have come to her door telling her that I have decided to leave. That little boy with my husband's last name has been in this world for three years, and ever since he has been in this world, I have been thinking of leaving.

"You know what, Rebecca? I never ask how you're doing or what's going on in your life. I always come in here talking about my problems, like you're my personal therapist. I'm sorry. How are you?"

She looks at me with her eyebrows raised. "I'm okay."

"Good. Congratulations on receiving such high recognition from your boss lady. That project is amazing. That project is going to help a lot of people."

Rebecca nods. "Thank you. The fact that it will help a lot of people is the reason we have worked so hard."

"So, I know you and your coworkers are going to celebrate. How are you going to celebrate?" She takes a deep breath as if she is trying to debate on whether or not she wants to tell me her plans. After a few minutes, she finally decides to share.

"Apryl has arranged for us to go to Jamaica for seven days."

"Jamaica? That's an expensive trip, sis."

"All expenses have been paid. The only thing I have to do is show up at the airport with my bags packed. Hell, I probably don't even need to pack anything." Rebecca smiles to herself, obviously trying to contain her excitement.

"That's wonderful. When are you leaving?"

My sister looks at her watch, "In approximately 27 hours."

"Wow, have you started packing yet?"

"That's what Temple and I were talking about. I know she has clothes with tags on it in her closet that I can fit. We won't have to go shopping at all."

The last phrase she says reminds me that Temple is apart of Apryl Simmons team. Although, I have turned green with envy, I manage to smile.

"I'm happy for you, Rebecca."

"Thanks. I'm surprised Cairo hasn't extended the same invitation to you. If it wasn't for Evans Construction joining us, none of this would be possible. I think you worked just as hard as us, sis."

Managing to keep a tight smile, I lie when I tell her Cairo just hasn't been able to get in contact with me yet. Contrary to what Rodney believed, Cairo had already thanked me for my hard work.

He had shown his gratitude by writing me a check for 2500 dollars. I'm sure this is enough money for me to join them on their little trip to Jamaica. Even though he has paid me for my hard work, it isn't the same as sending me on an all-expense paid, seven-day trip out of the country. Nor is it the same as giving me recognition for my hard work on a nationally televised show, in front of millions of people.

"Well, let me allow you to finish packing. Congratulations again and have fun."

"Thank you. Kiss the kids for me and hang in there, sis. I can't imagine how you must feel knowing there is someone else out there who was close enough to Rodney to have a baby with him. I can't sit here and tell you to get over it. I know it's hard. But you know what, sis? you guys have made it this far. You two love each other. I know he is sorry for his mistake. You guys will get through this."

With my ears burning now, I turn around to go out the door. I don't know how anyone could justify someone cheating as a mistake. The person who cheated made the choice to cheat, plain and simple. If I had been closer to my sister, I would pour out my heart to her and tell her I can't stay with Rodney isn't because of his betrayal. If I had been closer to my sister, I would tell her that I can't stay with him because I betrayed him long ago with my heart. But she wouldn't understand, I'm sure of it.

"Good night, Rebecca. Let me know if you need me to do anything before you go or while you're gone. I don't mind."

"Thank you." She stands at the door to see me out. Before I even pull out of the driveway, she has turned her back and closed the door.

## Temple

The island of Jamaica is so beautiful. I slept much of the flight so I would be fresh for when I arrived. There are so many things I want to do, so many things I want to see. The Seven mile beach of Negril is so beautiful, I can't think of anything better than putting on a two piece swimsuit to go enjoy the sun. When I voiced that that is all I wanted to on the first day, Becca let me know she wasn't having it. "I have already booked a spa package for you and I."

"Girl, we didn't come all this way to be lazy!"

"Really, Becca?"

The way she has placed her hands on her hips is almost comical. To keep from laughing, I cover my mouth until I can control myself.

"No one is trying to be lazy. I am just trying to relax. We have seven days to enjoy all that this resort, this beach, this island has to offer."

She looks at me blankly. "Temp, let's just be real for a second. As soon as you feel comfortable enough with

Cairo Evans, I doubt you and I will be seeing much of each other."

"Honey, please."

"Watch, I should bet you."

She and I chatter happily while going up to our hotel suite. On the way there, I run into Cairo and his sister, who are also about to enter their suites. My eyes take in the expanse of his muscular chest through the fitted shirt he is wearing. Taking in a deep breath, I finally look at his handsome face to find a perfectly, crooked smile. His white teeth shine like pearls against his brown skin.

"Good afternoon, Temple, Rebecca. Nice to see that you made it." His voice is so rich, my stomach clinches, reminding me that I haven't eaten. Or better yet, I haven't been fed, literally.

"Good afternoon, Cairo and Ivory. Yes, we made it. This island is so beautiful." I gush.

Ivory wiggles her fingers at us then she continues her trek toward the suite.

"What are your plans this afternoon?" Cairo queries with a hint of a smile.

"My good friend Becca here, booked us a spa package. So, an hour from now, we will be sprawled out across someone's table."

Cairo nods.

"Sounds like you all are in for a treat then. Have you decided about dinner?"

His expression conveys expectance. Maybe he is expecting me to say no and I do.

"No, I haven't decided on much of anything to be honest."

"Would you like to have dinner on the beach? Say, around 6?"

In my mind I think, maybe this dinner that we are going to have tonight will make this thing official, whatever it is. I've never been one into casual dating. At 26 years old, I really don't have the interest of getting to know someone if it doesn't serve a purpose in my life if that makes sense. Thinking of the possibility, I smile back at him. "Sure, I would love to."

"Then I will see you on the beach at 6."

"See you."

He nods at us before he turns to join his sister. As soon as he as out of earshot, Becca squeals like a little kid.

"I'm so happy for you!"

And right now, I am so happy for myself.

"Wow, what am I going to wear?"

We both crack up laughing because this had been the first thing I asked before I was scheduled to have dinner with him to talk about business. "I don't know, honey. This ain't business, this is pleasure in Jamaica." Becca slides her tongue past her lips, then flicks her tongue toward me. Elbowing her gently before I hook my arm inside the crook of her elbow as we walk down the hallway toward our suite.

Becca and I have a suite that is adjoined. Although the room is adjoined, we still have separate bathrooms and a beautiful view of the beach. "I am in love. I can't say I have ever been on a vacation to tell you the truth. " This I admit to Becca. By definition, I really had just taken time off work. This right here, this luxury, this foreign space, this feeling is wonderful causing me to smile. "Look at this, this is beautiful. Seven days is not enough."

"I know, right," Becca agrees with me as we both stand looking out at the beach from the ceiling to floor view of the sliding glass. After we place our bags into the closets provided. Then we head down to the parlor of the resort to have our massages.

Becca and I began talking with each other while the nail technicians are giving us mani and pedicures. But as soon as the masseuse began to knead our muscles between their fingers, making us both feel like we were on a planet other than earth, we stopped talking because our mouths had become slackened. In fact, I will admit I am the first to fall into a deep slumber. My slumber is so deep Becca accuses me of snoring. The fact that I feel so refreshed I don't even bother to debate her. When we go back up to the suite, I have to decide what I will wear to dinner, beachside with Cairo. Deciding on a pale yellow sundress that reaches my feet, I am glad I had the French manicure because my toes look cute displayed by my simple brown slides.

"Are you getting excited?"

"No, not really."

"Girl, why not? You might be having dinner on the beach with the man of your dreams in less than thirty minutes. Let me go ahead and tell you, I am the maid of honor and I will be in charge of everything that doesn't involve the groom." My friend makes me laugh again at how serious she is right now. When I give her a hug, she doesn't expect it.

"I'm so glad to have a friend like you, but girl, don't start planning my wedding before there is even a proposal. Don't jinx me."

"Ahhhh! So, you agree. He might be the one." Instead of replying, I decide to go down to the beach to wait for Cairo. To my surprise, Cairo is already walking along the beach. He is wearing long beige shorts and a beige button-down that is open. As it blows, I can see the definition of his strong chest again, and the soft curly hairs speckled across the width of his chest. Quietly, I trek across the sand to stand next to him. When he fills my presence beside him, he turns to look down at me. "Temple."

"Cairo." His name rolls off my tongue like the soft breeze blowing off the blue waters of the ocean. As the scent of sweet salt serenades my senses, I smile up at him.

"Would you like to walk?"

"Why yes, I would love to walk along the beach. You must have read my mind."

He places his hands in his pockets, then we slowly begin to walk along the beach.

Quietly at first, just enjoying the sights and sounds surrounding us. After several minutes of saying nothing, he finally turns to me, "So, Temple, tell me about yourself."

"Hmmm, I don't know where to begin."

"Start from the beginning. I want to know everything there is to know about Temple."

So, I started from the beginning. "My name is Temple. I'm 26 years old, and I'm from the large but small city of Virginia. I have two brothers, Tobias and

Trey, and I'm a daddy's girl. My father made sure I know how a man is supposed to treat a woman; he spoils me and my mother like second nature. I came to love Broadway plays and ballets. I prefer reading a good book over going out to socialize, but I socialize because it's a huge part of the career I chose. Uhhh, I moved to California because I wanted to try my hand at success with Apryl Simmons.

When I moved here, I didn't have anybody, except my ex. Now, I have a best friend named Rebecca that I love like a sister. I wouldn't trade her for anything in this world. I want to play the role of enhancing the quality of people's lives, be it through working with Apryl Simmons or on my own. And lastly, I love the thought of being in love. What about you? Tell me, who is Cairo Evans?"

The way he looks at me makes me feel like maybe I've shared too much. Yet, what he says lets me know I've said just enough to make him want to know more.

"I'm Cairo Evans, I was born and raised in Oakland, California. I'm a momma's boy 'til the day I die. It hurt me so bad to lose her. I thought by making sure her bills were paid, and she wanted for nothing, even though I didn't have anything to say to her, that would be enough to sustain our relationship. Foolishly, I called myself punishing her for the mistake she had made, instead of recognizing she has been paying for her mistake since the day before she made it. Now that she's gone, I regret that I didn't call her in the mornings just to hear her voice. I regret the days I didn't answer when she called me. I have custody of my kid sister Ivory. She is also my heart and I would do anything in this world to keep her safe. In this past six months, I've learned how precious time is. And I don't want to waste any time if I can help it. When you walked into the restaurant, that was the beginning of me opening my eyes to the possibility of so many things."

 Sighing, I try my best to set aside the fluttering I feel in my stomach as a reaction to the things he is saying to me is something I've longed to hear from the man that had my heart. But I try to play it off as if what he said has no effect on me.

"Like the possibility of working with Apryl Simmons and being able to help so many people?" He smiles.

"Yes, and the possibility of meeting a woman I can spend the rest of my life with. A woman who shares my interests and is just as ambitious as myself. Let me tell you something, I wasn't looking, but when you came, something said *hey man, that's her.*"

The skin of my cheeks flush with warmth. I have never been one to blush so much, yet here I am in his presence blushing every time he says something flattering. Maybe the average person wouldn't think the things he speaks to me are flattering. Either because they've heard it before or they don't believe the person speaking. For the last two years, I had been in a relationship that wasn't really. Aaron had been absent until it was convenient for him. Now, this man who is speaking to me has nothing to gain from feeling my head with lies. And my heart wants to believe him.

We don't have dinner until nine o'clock. From six to nine, we walk and talk. He and I even witnessed a couple get married. The ceremony is so lovely. The bride is just beautiful standing in her white dress covered in a pattern of lace with little pearls intricately placed in a way that reflects the setting sun. Listening to them repeat vows to each other that are meant to last a forever brings tears to my eyes. Cairo watches me, and at some point, he reaches for my hand, so we walk hand in hand anditfeels like it is meant to be this way.

**Stephanie**

This last week, I have been preparing myself to move out of the home I have shared with my husband for the last fifteen years—thoughts of him moving his mistress and their son cross my mind. However, I need to think about me. Taking the vacation time Cairo has given me has been a good thing. The bonus makes it better. Because I am meeting with a lady who will be showing me a house this evening. While waiting for her to arrive, I log into Facebook. The first notification that catches my attention comes from my sister's page. She has a new photo captioned "family." One thing I know about my sister is that she is very particular about what she posts. In fact, she wouldn't want anyone to know about her trip until after she is back. This photo of her, her little friend Temple, Cairo, and another young girl has me dialing her number. "Heyy!" I put on a façade through the phone as if I am calling her on a note of pleasantry when I am really calling to find out what in the hell Cairo is doing in Jamaica with them.

"Hey, Stephanie. Is everything okay?"

"Of course, I'm okay. I'm calling to see how you're doing. The picture you posted looks like you are having a ball. Have you met anyone?"

"Please, I didn't come a thousand miles away from home to meet anyone."

I picture her with one hand on her hip as she holds the phone with her other hand.

"Well, okay. I hope you don't push a man away if you should happen to meet one." Clearing my throat. I decide to cut straight to the chase. "I didn't know you knew Cairo well enough to be taking photos with him and call him family."

My sister sighs before giving me a short and snippy response. "I was actually referring to Temple when I captioned the pic family. And you're right, I don't know Cairo like that, but he's here."

Instead of addressing her snippiness, I decide to press for more information on Cairo. Just knowing that she is already aggravated with me, I know she is going to give me the information I seek in a hurry just to get me off the phone.

"Is Apryl Simmons there? Did you guys turn your vacation into a business trip?"

"No and no. Stephanie, what's going on with the third degree and the twenty-one questions?"

"Well, I am a little worried, because I haven't heard a thing from Cairo in almost a week."

"Stephanie, the man is on vacation. I thought you were too. Have you decided on your new house yet?" As much as I want to believe I hear interest in my sister's voice, I know better. She and I have never been close. In our mid to late twenties, I don't expect for her to even appear interested now.

"I'm about to look at a property right now. I thought I would be able to get Cairo's input. You know see what he thinks."

"Umm, why are you concerned about what Cairo thinks? Why would he even have an opinion about where you live anyway?"

The tone of my sister's voice suddenly starts to bother me. With attitude, I reply," He's been my boss for five years. I don't know about your boss, but mine cares about my wellbeing, and I am thankful that he cares."

"Stephanie, you're right, he is your boss. It's only right that he cares, but the way you sound right now makes me believe that you are obsessed with your boss."

"Obsessed?"

"Yes. Obsessed, that means. To preoccupy or fill the mind continually and to a troubling extent. You shouldn't be worried about Cairo, because I don't think he is the least bit worried about you right now."

"What is that supposed to mean?"

"Read between the lines, hun. Kiss my nieces for me. Goodnight." My sister doesn't even wait for my response before she hangs up. With that, I am not at all happy with her labeling me as obsessed with anyone. Caring about someone doesn't mean you are obsessed by any means. Rolling my eyes, I place my cell phone back in my bag right when I see the real estate agent pull into the driveway beside me. Just a few minutes ago, I had been excited about seeing this new place just for me. I have been thinking of the possibility of having candlelight dinners with Cairo seated across from me. And just having these thoughts alone, put me on cloud nine. I had been singing the old school hit by Olivia all morning...

*You came and took my breath away, I was caught in a vine at a time in the night where my life wasn't right, but then again suddenly, suddenly you came, and I was swept away. Ooh like a bird, I just fly cause I'm free. Free to laugh, free to love, free to be. No rain comes down on me. This is what's happening, floating all the time on cloud nine.*

    Three years ago, when Cairo allowed me to cry on his shoulder, although he didn't have to. He could have sent me home to grieve over my marriage for the day, but he let me stay and cry until I couldn't cry anymore. Cairo had been a gentleman. He ordered lunch for me and made sure I ate. What took the cake for me as he drove me home. At the front door, he pulled me into his arms, and the thing that took the cake for me is that Rodney had been peeking out the window, and he witnessed it all. He even opened the door and stood there as Cairo released me from his hold. Cairo didn't acknowledge him.

The look he gave him measured him up as a man, and it looked like he came up with nothing.

After that, Rodney hated for me to go to work. He hated for me to mention anything about work, and to spite him, I always brought home my work. During that time, I found so much to love about the man who employs me. Now I am ready to admit I am in love with him, but he's off on a beach with white sand and my sister. And my sister's cute best friend, Temple.

All throughout the tour of the property, I had nothing on my mind except the photo on my sister's Facebook page, captioned "Family."

## Cairo

Our seven-day vacation turned in to ten days. I was able to convince Temple to stay with me three more days while her friend decided to head home to help her sister. It's funny how I am just now learning after all the time that Stephanie, my assistant has been working with me that Becca is her younger sister. Both women are polar opposites indeed. Becca is quiet and reserved when Stephanie is loud and demanding.

As we ride with Becca to the airport, I overhear Becca telling Temple that she had better come home with some good news. The moment Temple cuts her eyes at me, I know they must be talking about me, so I walk away, giving them a little privacy. After they hug, I hear Temple tell Becca that she had better let her know when she makes it back home. If I didn't know any better, I would say Temple is a little saddened to see her friend leave. So, I make it a point to make sure the rest of the time she spends in Jamaica that she won't have time to miss her.

A few hours later, Temple is lounging on the beach in a white one-piece bathing suit. The suit shows off the thickness of her mocha brown thighs and the voluptuousness of the rest of her body.

 The remainder of our time is spent riding horses along the beach. Temple admits she has never ridden or even touched a horse. It happened to be a first-time experience for my sister as well. Me, I have ridden before. My mother's uncle owned a small ranch in the state of Washington. Three summers straight, my mother sent me to him for the summer, and he taught me how to ride and care for his horses. Just like riding a bike, it's something that never leaves you. I could easily tell the horses had been trained to go a certain distance, move at a certain pace. Ivory took the reins just like she has been on the saddle before, and she was eager to take the trip across Seven-Mile beach. However, I can tell from the look in Temple's eyes that she is nervous. So, I make sure I stay close to her. When she relaxes, she smiles at me. "I appreciate you. You know you could be up there with your sister." She nods her head forward in my sister's direction, where she is at the front of the group.

"Ivory is good, she is where she wants to be and so am I."

When the ride is over, after I get off my horse and help Temple off the saddle Temple gently pats the side of her horse's neck.

"Thank you for going easy with me, Ginger." Ginger looks the opposite of the way you'd expect her to look. She is white with greyish spots and a coal black mane. Just beautiful. Offering Temple my hand as we walk away from the stable, the tour guide stops us. "Would you like to take a picture, madam? Sir?"

Temple looks to me to see if I agree when she nods her head, and I nod my head in agreement. She smiles at me shyly as I take the opportunity to pull her closer to me. The tour guide snaps the picture. It only takes a few seconds for it to develop. He hands it to Temple, nodding his head. "Very nice, enjoy the rest of your stay."

"Wow, it's beautiful. Thank you."

"You are so welcome," he says in a heavy but crisp accent.

"Thank you for having me as your guest."

"Thank you for being my guest. I have truly enjoyed you and learned a lot."

In the distance, I see my sister walking toward us. She is holding a picture in her hand as well.

"Okay, Cairo, I think I would like to talk to you about making a little investment."

Before she tells me what it is, I think I already know, and so does Temple. We both chuckle at my sister. She skips beside me with a big smile on her face.

"You're laughing, but I am so serious."

"I hear you, Ivory. A horse would be a great investment. Let me think about how I can make that happen." Her mouth drops open and she squeals lightly, just before skipping to the other side of Temple.

"I want you to stay around. Honey, you are a great influence on my brother."

This time we all share a laugh. Sometime during our vacation, I notice that Temple and Ivory forged a relationship.

When we weren't participating in an activity on the beach or at the resort, Ivory, Temple, and Becca found something to do together. When I have glimpsed Ivory looking at Temple with admiration, I am confident that I have made a good choice to follow my intuition. My mind had already started to tell my heart that she is surely the one.

The second night after the departure of Becca, Temple and I attend a theme party, where we sit up under a canopy while the breeze blows off the ocean. We watch fire eaters and limbo dancers as we drink Island Margaritas and eat traditional Jamaican food, like callaloo, ackee, and saltfish. A live band plays a catchy Caribbean beat that has Temple dancing against me. I place my arms around her as I move with her.

"I'm so glad you invited me," she whispers against my ear, flicking her tongue purposely against my earlobe. This little action causes me to shudder while pulling her closer.

"Me too." I lean down so that my lips are in line with her ear, nipping softly to give her the same feeling of pleasure she had just given me. If I'm not mistaken, I think I hear her growl just before my lips meet hers in a soft, yet hungry kiss. This one kiss would have lasted all night if she didn't pull away, I'm sure of it. I feel for her in my loins. I already feel for her in my heart, as I have felt for her in my mind since day one.

"Cairo, I want to trust you. I really do."

"Then trust me." When I kiss her this time, I leave her breathless.

"I don't want you to hurt me. I can't be hurt again." Her fear is plausible. I witnessed how her last boyfriend had betrayed her, and if that wasn't enough, he embarrassed her by letting his side piece throw a drink in her face. That incident has never come up between us, but I know his betrayal has a lot to do with her feelings of distrust.

As flames light the beach up, the reflection of the oranges from the flames reflect in her bright eyes. Right then, I know she is the last person on this earth next to my sister that I'll ever hurt or allow to be hurt.

"I'm making you a promise tonight. I won't hurt you."

"How do I know that's not just the liquor talking?"

Placing my finger beneath her chin, I turn her head slightly so she can see the table where we had been sitting. The only drink I had ordered all night is on the table, the glass is still full like the server had just placed it there, instead of thirty or so minutes ago. Maybe it has been more.

"I don't allow liquor or anything else to speak for me." After I place a kiss to her forehead, she gently drops her head to my chest. And there it remains as we move together along with the melodic sounds coming from the band. It feels right to know I am holding my future. This I am sure of.

It is a little past one a.m. when I walk Temple back to her room. At this point, I can tell she is a little more than tipsy. She is touchy, and when I say that, I mean she clings to me like a second skin if I didn't have my clothes on. And the fact that she trusts me to be in her personal space says a lot about this trip. I have made more progress with her in nine days than I have ever attempted to make it with anyone else in months. Something is telling me that this means a lot for our future. Handing me the keycard for her suite, she watches me with heavily lidded eyes as if she is about to pass out. However, she surprises me. When I turn the knob to push the door open, she places her hand over mine before she gently pulls me inside behind her.

"Stay with me."

Turning the lock on the door behind me, I follow her. She has the blinds pushed open so there is a nice view of the ocean. The view is absolutely captivating from where I am standing. Even though my suite is nicely positioned with a straight path to the beach from the patio, the view is breathtaking from where I am standing in her suite.

Temple steps around me to walk toward the closet, where she has her clothing hanging. I see her reach for what looks like an oversized shirt, and I assume she is going to put it on. I watch her until she disappears into the bathroom, and then I hear the shower start to run. When she comes out, she is wearing the large shirt which reaches well past her knees, and she has a towel wrapped around her head.

"Feel free to take a shower as well. Oh, you know what? I forgot you don't have anything to wear."

"If you don't mind, I will go up to my suite, check on my sister in her suite, then grab some clothes, and I'll come right back."

"I don't mind."

After placing a soft kiss on the side of her face, I take my cell phone and everything except the keycard to my suite out of my pockets and then place them on the dark oak dresser with the large mirror. "Be back in a minute."

She watches me walk out the door. I walk swiftly up the hall to my suite just to retrieve a pair of boxers, my jogger pajama pants, and t-shirt even though I only sleep in the pants. I also grab something to wear for when I awake and am ready to spend my last day in Jamaica exploring the remaining sights that I have yet to tap into. I am hoping to have Temple by my side.

Picking up the phone, I call my sister to check on her. When she answers, I tell her to open her door, so I can lay my eyes on her.

"Big brother, it's late. Where have you been?" Ivory crosses her arms against her chest while waiting for my explanation. She makes me smile, because she is doing her best to imitate me, and she is doing a very good job at it.

"Temple and I were on the beach, dancing and watching them eat fire, while the live band played some good ole reggae."

"Aww, I heard the band from up here. They sounded awesome. So, I see you are enjoying your time with Temple."

"Absolutely."

"I like her a lot. I think she's good for you."

Nodding my head, I tell my sister good night, even though it is now well into the wee hours of the morning. "Good night, big brother. I love you."

"Love you too, sis. If you need me, I'll be with Temple."

The way my sister smiles at me, knowingly. I shake my head because I know what must be going through her mind. "Ohhh. Well, alright."

"Nah, sis. She means more to me than that."

"Awesome. My big brother is growing up," she says jokingly.

"Go to bed, girl."

She waves me off before going back to her bed.

Not even five minutes later, I return to Temple's suite. She is laying on the lounge chair in front of the window reading a book. Quietly, I start the shower. When I come out, she is still seated on the lounge chair. She tells me to have a seat beside her.

Temple places the book on the little wicker table beside her as she turns to look up at me. "I think the ocean is just beautiful at night."

"It is, have you ever taken a ride on a boat along the river at night? This right here just makes you appreciate the beauty of the water even more."

"No, I haven't. But yes, I can see why it would make you appreciate natures beauty more."

We sit quietly, just listening the sound of the waves crashing against the shore. Soon I hear Temple snoring lightly, I pat her hand to rouse her.

"Let's go inside." As soon as we are inside, we lay across the bed. When Temple gets under the covers, I politely get on top of them next to her then pull her closer to me. "Sweet dreams Temple."

"Good night, Cairo." And we fall asleep as I inhale the thick scent of her.

## Temple

The incessant ringing of my phone awakens me. At first, I am disoriented, forgetting that the arms of the man who has re-awakened my heart to love quicker than I anticipated, are wrapped around me. And I also forget that I am waking up in Jamaica. Rubbing my eyes and stretching, I reach for my cellphone, but it stops only to ring again. Looking down at the display, I see that the caller is my brother Tobias. I also see text messages from my mother and my brother Trey. This causes my heart to drop, because I know something must be wrong.

"Temple, where are you? We need you to come home now!" my brother shouts into the phone making me sit completely up at the side of the bed. The remnants of sleep have left me, and I have become excited.

"What's wrong, Tobias?" I don't realize I'm shaking and shouting until I feel a gentle touch on my back that does very little to calm me yet lets me know I'm not alone.

"It's dad, they had to airlift him to the hospital. Temple, we don't know what happened. He was doing alright, he just collapsed."

"Oh no. Oh no."

"We have been trying to call you."

"I'm sorry I was sleeping. I'm in Jamaica, but I'm on my way." Hurriedly, I stumble toward the closet to gather my clothes and throw them into my carryon bags. By now, Cairo is standing behind me with a look of concern on his face.

"Okay, sis. Get here as soon as you can."

"Tobias, where's my mom?" It concerns me that he hadn't mentioned her or maybe he had. My mind has become a mess in less than five minutes.

"She's here. The doctor had to give her something to help her relax, but she's here. Get here soon, sis. Are you alone?"

"No, no," I stutter, "I'm not alone." The quietness on the other end of the phone tells me that my brother is waiting for an explanation. Quickly I decide there is no time for secrecy or even worrying about anything besides getting to my father. "Cairo is here."

"Cairo? Yo, let me speak to him."

With some reluctance, I pass the phone to Cairo. He doesn't question who is on the phone; he just accepts it and places it directly to his ear. After he said yes a few times, I suppose to confirm that we are indeed together in Jamaica and a few "no worries, I'll make sure she's good," Cairo puts the phone on the dresser. At first, I feel like I am moving in slow motion then again, I'm not sure what I'm doing.

"Hey, calm down. I'm going to arrange a flight that will get you to your family, alright. You won't have to worry about anything except getting on the plane and going straight there, alright?"

"Are you sure? I haven't even looked at flights." While I am rambling, Cairo pulls me into his arms as if he is pulling a sheet from the dryer to fold.

"Calm down, alright."

"But my dad-"

"Go take a shower, get dressed, I'll take care of everything else." When he finally lets me go after a few minutes, I go do as he suggests with a small thought of the reason why I never allowed anyone else to do something else for me besides my parents. The reason being they either failed horribly or didn't attempt at all.

Nine and a half hours later, I am landing at the airport. And just as he promised, Cairo had someone pick me up from the airport then take me straight to my family at the hospital. When I arrive, I didn't know what to expect, although my brothers made it a point to keep me updated on my father's condition.

Trey meets me in the lobby. The first thing he does is envelope me in his arms. "Please tell me he's okay." After a few minutes pass and he still hasn't answered me, I pull away from him to look up into his eyes.

"Trey, what's going on?" He still doesn't answer me, so I pull away so I can go find out myself. But he holds on to my arms even tighter.

"Trey, no. I want to see him." Now I am in the lobby of the hospital sounding like a scared little girl. I continue to try pulling away until Tobias appears in the lobby.

"Sis, calm down, he's in surgery. It was touch and go for a while. Right now that's all I know."

"What happened?"

"He was mowing grass and just collapsed. The neighbors rushed to him. The paramedics said if they hadn't given him CPR when they did, he wouldn't…" suddenly my brother chokes up. He hits the air and walks away from us. Tobias has always been the strength of our family right next to our dad. To see him falling apart right now causes me to break down in tears in Trey's arms. It is Trey that says something to make us pull it together.

"Listen, I know this is scary right now, but we have got to show strength for mommy. You know she isn't taking this well at all. We have got to be strong for her. Temp, do you hear me?" He places his fingers under my chin to make me look at him. "Do you hear me, sis? We have got to be strong. Daddy told us to always be strong."

And in that moment, I feel like my brother and I are kids again, lost in the park waiting for Tobias to find us before some perverted stranger did. Jamaica is far from my mind, so is the successes I had just celebrated. Mentally, I beat myself up, feeling like I should have gone home to celebrate with my family. Maybe if I had gone home, my dad would have skipped mowing the grass. Instead, he would watch boxing with me or we would have played cards. I don't know exactly what we would be doing, but I'm sure he would be okay.

## Stephanie

When Becca came back from her trip, she had agreed to babysit the kids while I pack my belongings. So alone at my house, I have made some great progress. I have even pulled a lot of my things to the front door, so they would be easily accessible. Rodney has been quiet ever since I told him that I plan to move out. Tonight, he has been pacing the floors, and I have been watching him, while he is watching me. Suddenly, when he stops to look at me, the bass from his voice causes me to jump. It's not that I haven't ever heard that tone of voice from him, it's that he speaks so suddenly. While he is speaking, he is stepping closer to me; this causes me alarm.

"I'm sorry for everything, Stephanie. That woman doesn't mean anything to me. We were going through something, you and I. I couldn't talk to you, so I fell for what she was trying to give me."

No matter how apologetic he seems, I just can't get past his betrayal.

"Rodney, you had a baby with another woman, that's not something I can just get over." Just the thought of the intimacy they shared causes me to tear up. Maybe I hadn't been the best wife, but I didn't deserve to be cheated on. No matter how long it's been, I just can't accept it. Shaking my head as I back away from him, the wall behind me stops me from moving any further.

Suddenly he pulls me into his arms, forcing me to look at him. Of course, I am resisting him with my forearms pressed against his chest, pushing him back. But Rodney is solid. No matter how hard I push, he's not budging.

"I can't let you just walk out of my life and give up on us."

"Rodney, let me go. You are the one who gave up when you stepped out, slept with a woman unprotected, and had a child. I'm leaving and there is nothing you can do to stop me." Taking a huge breath, I push him back with all my might. Rodney is solid, so he barely moves. When I look into his eyes, I notice this crazed expression that scares me. He tightens his grip around me, pulling me closer and tighter against him. The smell of liquor wafts around us, and just as I had previously feared, I'm sure he has been drinking. Liquor has been the fuel that causes him to do the most acting out, especially when he has been in the wrong.

"Stephanie, I'm not letting you take my children away from me."

"You don't have a choice, worry about your son and leave us alone. Mistake my ass." Soon we are in a full on shouting match. He tells me if I had been there for him, he wouldn't have stepped out. I haven't been willing to take the blame for it and I won't start today.

"Oh, oh, I get it. You must think that dude you work for is going to come riding his white horse to save you from the vows you took."

"You're talking crazy."

"No, I'm not talking crazy. I'm talking the truth. You really think that dude is trying to have anything to do with you outside of work? You don't think I see how you're keeping up with him?" His accusation are correct, but he's not supposed to be aware. All the feelings I have for Cairo, I have always believed I'd kept them hidden so well no one would notice.

"I'm not keeping up with anyone but my children here in this house, you bastard. You've done wrong, so you feel like you need to point a finger at me to get the heat off you."

Rodney laughs bitterly, causing a bad taste in my mouth.

"Stephanie, you're pining after a man who is taking other beautiful women to Jamaica. He chose who he wanted with him. The messed-up thing about it is, you've worked tirelessly for him for five years; he knows you deserved to go on a vacation just as much as anyone else. But he didn't choose you to go with him. He chose the beautiful woman he just met. What does that tell you? He don't care nothing about your washed-up ass. You don't mean any more to him than the next person on the street,"

Before I could catch myself, I grab the lamp on the end table next to where I'm pinned to the wall. And I try my best to hit him in the head with it. I've never wanted to physically hurt him more than I have at this very moment. When I swing the lamp, I miss his head. The glass shatters when it crashes against his chest. All the pieces fall at our feet. I need to get out of his space fast because I had tried to hurt him, and that is something we'd said we would never do after having experienced our share of domestic abuse in previous relationships. I am able to get out of the corner, but I don't get far before he grabs my hair, making my whole body halt.

"You're hurting me."

"You just tried to knock me out."

"I'm sorry."

"You know what though? I'm going to make you sorry that you ever decided to choose him over me."

All of a sudden, he just releases me and I stumble. As I'm trying to keep from falling on my face, Rodney walks past me swiftly. I don't know where he's going until I see him walk toward the table in the hallway. As soon as he moves to pull open the drawer, I know what he is about to reach for, the little 9mm that we keep there. While letting out a scream, I lunge toward him, hoping to stop him from getting the gun. However, he is prepared for me to do exactly what I had done. In one more swift motion, he swings his elbow back, hitting me in my stomach. The blow knocks the breath clean from my body and I double over in pain. Rodney is steadily reaching for the gun. Once again, I make a move to stop him. This time when I do, he pushes me down to the floor, gets on top of me, and begins to deliver open-handed slaps to my face repeatedly. My instincts make me fight back or at least I believe I am. All I end up with in the end is a bruised face and busted lip. With muddled thoughts, I'm thinking, I can't believe he hit me. When the doorbell rings, he gets off me and goes out the back door. I'm sure he has the gun in his hand, and I'm sure he is going to his car and straight to Cairo. The person at the door is my neighbor; she heard the commotion and came to see if we were okay. As soon as she sees my face, she offers to call the police, but I don't have my mind on my safety, all I can think about is whether or not Rodney is going for Cairo. I try to find my cell phone, which I know for a fact I had left on the kitchen counter by the back door.

"Oh no."

Grabbing my head as I cry out, "He took my phone." I already know he took my phone so he could easily contact Cairo and lure him somewhere.

"This is all my fault. I should have never made it seem like… I can't believe this is even happening to me right now."

"Honey, it's not your fault."

My middle-aged neighbor tries to sympathize with me. Although, I know she means well, I can't focus on what she's saying to me. It's my fault all this is happening, because I didn't leave when my heart and mind told me it was time to go. All I see is that this is my fault that Rodney is going after Cairo because I never should have made it worse by giving ANYBODY the inclination that I even think of my boss in a romantic way. Cairo has never come on to me or given me any reason to feel our working relationship could transform into anything else. Yes, if Rodney does anything to hurt Cairo, I'm blaming it all on myself. Remembering his cell phone number by heart is the best thing I could've ever done. Calling him to warn him that Rodney may be coming will prove to be the hardest task. If he is like every other person I know, he screens his calls. When an unknown number appears on his phone display, he won't bother to answer. At this very moment, I know I have never prayed so hard.

## Cairo

As soon as I'm sure my sister is okay at my home, I get on my private plane headed straight to VA because I feel the need to be by Temple's side. The helpless expression on her face before she got on the flight home made me feel helpless. Again, I have always been one to solve any problem that comes up around me. But this one is out of my control. And it bothers me so much I can barely think straight. The minute my plane lands, I power my phone on to discover several voicemails. Taking the time to listen because I thought the calls may be coming from Temple at the hospital, I discover not one of the messages are from Temple, but they are from my assistant Stephanie.

"Cairo, please pick up. Look, I don't know what's going on, but I think my husband may be coming to find you. Please call me as soon as you get this message. It's an emergency!" Immediately, I draw blanks in my mind as to why Stephanie's husband would be looking for me. But the second message tells me exactly why and it pisses me off. The last thing I have time for is to deal with a jealous husband who has no reason to be worried about me. I decide to handle her issue later as the taxi I hailed from the airport finally pulls up to the hospital where Temple and her family are. Stepping into the lobby of the hospital, Tobias is waiting for me. My friend of several years looks worried, and I feel sorry because there is nothing I can do to change the fact that his father is possibly clinging to his life while in the ICU.

"I'm sorry, man. Is there anything I can do?"

After giving him a handshake, he steps back, "Help comfort my sister, man. She is all in pieces. I'm trying to keep it together for our mom, but it's getting harder with every hour that he lays in there like he ain't gone wake up." Having suffered my own family loss recently, I try not to think about losing my mother, but I can relate to the way he's feeling.

"Where is she?" All I want to do is comfort the woman who exuded such vibrance the moment she stepped into my life.

"North tower, fourth floor."

Making the short trip to the elevator by following the

signs. Once I make it to the very quiet and private section of the North Tower, my eyes land on Temple, who is staring out the window. Her thick crown of hair is pulled back into a messy ponytail, and she is dressed in clothing that seems to swallow her up.

"Temple."

When I breathe her name just loud enough to reach her ears, she looks up. Now that she is wearing the look of sadness, trepidation, and worry, I can say I barely recognize the woman in front of me. I don't wait for an invitation to pull her into my arms, I invite myself, and she doesn't shy away. In fact, I accept the weight of her as she leans into me.

"Have you eaten?"

"I don't feel like eating."

"You need some nourishment. Come on, let's go to the cafeteria, grab some fruit or something." The word 'no' is written all over her face, so I add, "Your big brother is worried about you. You know it's a lot to worry about you and your mother. You have got to be strong, so you guys can lean on each other."

I feel her inhale, unsure about leaving for fear of missing something. When I look around us, I see a little map pointing toward the North Tower Cafe. When I make the suggestion and she discovers that we don't have to go far, she's not as reluctant to go. The whole time my cell phone vibrates in my pocket. I'm sure its Stephanie calling with her worries. After several minutes of constant vibrating, I finally excuse myself to answer her call.

"I'm so glad you answered. Where are you?"

"Will you tell me what's going on?"

"Rodney just destroyed every window, every sign and god knows what else at the office. He's trying to find out where you live. Where are you?"

"I'm handling some business right now. My insurance will take care of whatever damage he's caused at the office. You'd better stop him. If he goes anywhere near my home, he's going to be sorry. What the hell is going on anyway?"

After several minutes pass and she says nothing, I yell for her to tell me what's going on.

"I think he thinks that you and I are messing around."

"He what? What the hell would make him think that??"

When she begins to stutter, I become more upset, thinking about my sister being at home in harm's way if this lunatic should go there acting stupid. Here I am, over a thousand miles away.

"I don't know what's going on, but you know what, I don't have time to play. What's his full name so I can have his dumb ass picked up? Start talking fast before I have you picked up too."

"What?"

"As an accomplice, you told me this is happening because of you."

"Cairo, I'm sorry." I don't even wish I could say something to make her feel better.

"What's his name? What is he driving?"

As I'm waiting on her to give me the information, I notice Temple's other brother enter the cafe. I become pissed because right now, I want to be comforting Temple. Not on the phone talking this nonsense. I hear

Temple ask her brother if he is awake and can they see him. Then I see her walking toward me in a rush. I disconnect the call while Stephanie is still on the line apologizing,

"He's awake, Cairo. I'm going to go see him." And because I know they won't allow but so many visitors in ICU to begin with, I tell her that I'll be waiting for her in the lobby. She takes her brother's hand before they're out of my sight, and I notice the way he looks in my direction before they walk out of the cafe.

## Temple

To see my father lying in the hospital bed with ashen skin while hooked up to several machines causes me to become choked up. When I see my mother at his side, holding his hand, I hold my breath to keep the tears from falling.

"Heyyyy, Temp." To hear my father's normal booming voice sound so weak makes me even more sad. Through my tears, I attempt to smile as I take my dad's free hand in mine then kiss his warm knuckles.

"Heyyyy, daddy. I love you so much. Don't you ever leave me."

"I won't, baby girl."

"How are you feeling?" Holding his hand to my cheek as I wait for his reply, I notice my mother doing the same thing as me, shedding tears but holding the bulk of them back. Carefully, I reach across him for my mom's hand.

"Baby, your daddy is tired. I feel like I've been working out in the field for a week from sunup to sundown. I'm tired."

"So, you act out this way to get some rest? That's not fair, daddy. You scared us," I gently scold him. From what I've learned, he'd had a stroke, and only time will tell if he'll be able to function the way a healthy, sixty-five year old man would.

"No, baby, this wasn't a part of my plan."

"I know it wasn't, daddy. I know. I love you."

"I love you too, baby girl."

"Temp," he laughs dryly. "Temp. I love you, Temp."

"Trey is here. Tobias is here."

"And I heard that Temple's friend is here," my mom says unexpectedly. I look at her in surprise. She manages to smile at me.

"Who, Becky? Errr, Becca?"

"Becca's on the way."

"Oh, she is, coming all the way from California, huh? Well, I misunderstood. You say someone is here?"

Before I can respond, my mom begins to explain the arrival of Cairo. The friend she has yet to meet. "His name is Cairo Evans. He owns a huge, reputable construction company. We've been hearing many good things about him and his company. He came to give our baby some moral support. All the way from California."

"All the way from California, huh? Is that right, Temp?"

"Yes, daddy."

He nods his head up and down slowly. "I'm so glad to hear it."

When I see that his eyes begin to lower, I know that it's time to let him rest. "Well, If he's here to support my baby girl, I want to meet him."

I've always dreamed of having my dad meet my boyfriend, then have that boyfriend ask my dad for his blessing to marry me. This isn't the way I'd dreamed of it happening, even when I know it isn't going to happen.

"Okay, Daddy, get some rest."

"Well, where are my boys at?"

"They're outside, I'll send them in." After kissing my dad again, I slowly leave his room so I can send Trey and Tobias in. Tobias, Trey, and Cairo are seated on the couch beside the window.

"He's ready to see you now."

Both Tobias and Trey give me a hug before going to join our mother and dad. Leaving me alone with Cairo, who gives me a reassuring smile before asking, "How's he doing?"

"My dad is ready to meet my friend from California."

"Oh, okay. Really? So, your friend is coming?"

Shaking my head, I look at him, wondering what in the world he must be thinking, "Yeah, she's coming, but he was referring to my friend Cairo Evans. Funny, right? This came from my mother; can you believe that?"

Cairo gently touches my cheek, while looking into my eyes. "That's a big wow for me. I'm glad he's up talking. I'm even happier to see your smile." His comment makes me blush. Blushing is all I seem to do in his presence. Self-consciously, I look down to hide my blush. Not until he places his finger beneath my chin do I look up.

"Your smile is beautiful."

"Thank you and thank you for coming."

"You're welcome. So tell me about your dad and the rest of your family?"

He looks genuinely interested, so I begin, "Ah, my

dad loves boxing, a good game of spades, The Isley Brothers, Charlie Wilson, and fishing. And oh, did I say he absolutely loves the Isley Brothers and Charlie Wilson?" The fact that Cairo appears to be so attentive to every word I'm saying gives him so many points in my book. Our moment is interrupted when his phone rings. It is then when I remember how upset he seemed earlier.

"Is everything okay with Ivory?"

"Ivory's good. I just, uhh, have some bullcrap going on."

"You're a very busy man. When are you going to handle your business?"

Unexpectedly, Cairo pulls me into his arms. Then he looks down at me, "I have been handling business, making sure you and your fam are good."

"I'm good, Cairo. My family is here; you need to handle your business back in California."

"Again, my business is good back home. Right now, my concern is how everything is going with you."

Deciding not to debate with him any further, I remain quiet and allow him to remain by my side until my father is released from the hospital. Cairo even stays with me well after my father is all settled in. The longer he stays, the closer we become. He books a room at a nearby hotel even though my mother tells him he can stay in the guest bedroom of our family home. When he said he would stay to make sure I'm good, he stayed to make sure I am good. Every other weekend he would fly to California to visit me and my family. One weekend he surprised my dad with a concert starring The Isley Brothers and Charlie Wilson.

"You know you really didn't have to do this."

We watch my mother and father dance as the group sing a tune they remember from when they were younger. Cairo smiles down at me, showing off his pearl white teeth.

"I know I didn't have to do it, but I could, so I wanted to."

Tobias and his wife walk over to where we are standing. Tobias opens his hand to offer Cairo a handshake, which Cairo accepts. "Thanks, man. My mom and dad are enjoying themselves so much, I think we are going to have to send them off to get a room."

My mother is looking up into my dad's eyes with a dreamy look while he holds her tightly by the waist. Observing them, I can't recall a time when I have seen them so relaxed and enjoying each other.

"I think it has a lot to do with Temple being home," Tobias comments.

Apryl Simmons has allowed me to work from my parents' home in VA as long as I feel the need to. It's been three months.

"You know I think so too," his wife states looking from me to Cairo. I'm not sure how to label what we are. This man has traveled over a thousand miles to see me every other weekend for the last three months. And we have only kissed.

"I wonder if I should be worried. I will be heading back soon." I know that my boss is allowing me to work remotely from the kindness of her heart. Now that my dad is better, I think it is time to go back to my life.

"No, you can't worry, sis. Soon, he will have a rbrand-new granddaughter to spoil. You should make sure you come home to visit more often though. We don't want you to be jealous off all the attention the new girl is getting." Tobias's wife swats his arm as we all laugh at my brother's joke. Later on that night before Cairo heads to his hotel room, we sit on the back post of my parents' house.

"Do you remember the first time we sat watching the sunset?"

"Yes, in good ole Jamaica," I reply to Cairo's question with a smile, reminiscing.

"I can get used to watching every sunset with you, you know?"

"Really? I think I'd like that."

"No matter where we are."

"Are you saying that because of what my brother said about my dad?"

"Yes, I wanted you to know I would come to you wherever you are."

I suppose you could say he seals his words with a kiss. It seems like minutes before we move apart. The energy that we have now is something I hope we will keep when we both are back to our reality.

## Stephanie

The cops picked Rodney up after he damaged Cairo's property. He was on his way to Cairo's house when he was picked up. I should be happy that Cairo didn't fire me the night I had called him, because this wouldn't have happened if it weren't for me. For the last few months, he has been in and out of this office so quickly, I haven't had the chance to say more than a few words to him. I've glanced him just long enough to say he doesn't look the same. I don't know what it is, but I can tell he is not the same Cairo that he was before he won that award for the project he had completed with Apryl Simmons. He hadn't been the same since his trip to Jamaica.

When I mention the trip to my sister, she becomes so upset with me. I almost expect her to hit the roof. "You know, Stephanie haven't you done enough? Shouldn't you just be going on about your life and stop worrying about other people? Especially Cairo Evans?"

"Whoa, why are you tripping? Let me find out you want him for yourself." Although I know what I am saying is the furthest thing from the truth, I figure if I continue to aggravate her, she will undoubtedly tell me what I want to know.

"Please. You're miserable, Stephanie. I don't know what snapped in your head when you found out Rodney cheated, but you really need to consider getting some help." Becca looks at me with disgust. This look is foreign. Normally she looks at me as if she felt sorry for me. I don't want her pity or disgust. The last thing I expected was for her to make this remark, so it catches me off guard. I had come to her apartment without an invitation, so there is no real reason for me to be here.

"You might be right, sister. You might be right." This is all I say as I leave her standing in the middle of her living room. Still not satisfied with my life without Cairo. As I stand outside on Rebecca's front step, I hear my sister receive a call.

"Hey, girl!! I miss you. Nothing's been the same at the office. I'm almost jealous because Apryl is walking around like she can't get it together all because she doesn't have her whole team. Are you on your way back? Wow, you're already here? Open the door; I'm coming over. I need details about the whole Cairo Evans experience." Hearing his name makes my antennae go up and all I want to do is listen for more. But when I don't hear my sister talking anymore, I automatically assume she has gone to another room of the house. I am shocked as ever when my sister opens her front door with her keys in her hand and purse on her shoulder. She looks at me with a surprised expression.

"Uhhh, excuse me, what are you still doing here? Can I help you with something?"

"Oh, no. I-I thought I dropped something."

We just stand looking at each other without saying anything at all until she holds both of her hands up, "Well, did you find it, Stephanie?"

"Yeah, yeah, I got it." And that's the truth, because as I stood eavesdropping, I learned something new. I'd suspected Cairo has taken an interest in my sister's best friend when I have been the one on his side.

"Well, okay then. Kiss my nieces for me." Becca walks past me to get to her car. There are so many things I should do. I should walk away and mind my business because who Cairo decides to see is none of mine. But I can't. As soon as I get in my car, I dial his number. It doesn't matter that it's past eight p.m. and it doesn't matter that I don't know what I will say when I call him. I call him anyway.

"Yeah."

His tone is gruff like he doesn't want to be bothered. Still, I hold the phone close to my ear, as if something will change.

"I was just calling to check on you. You know it's been a while." I can't hide the hopefulness in my tone. As I look in the rearview mirror at my sister reversing out of her parking space, the definition of obsessed comes to mind. Then I begin to think about the ways I might consider myself obsessed.

"It's been a while for what? I really don't need you to check in on me. You're my assistant. You punch my clock five days a week from 9 to 5. I think you need to take some more time off."

"What? What do you mean, Cairo?"

He exhales loudly into the phone before finally

replying.

"I think you need to take some time off. I will pay you another month's salary while you look for other employment. I won't do this with you anymore. After everything, I'd be a fool to."

It takes a few minutes for what he has just said to me to register in my brain. When I realize, Cairo has basically just told me that he is letting me go, I become a babbling fool.

"But wait, I don't mean any harm. You know I just moved out on my own, there is no way I will find a job that pays me what you have paid me,"

"Like I said, I don't think this is going to work. I'll leave the check with the receptionist Monday morning."

"Cairo, no-" Before I can get my full sentence out, he disconnects the call, and I am left sitting in front of my sister's house looking and feeling like a fool.

## Temple

"So, you're telling me in the last three and a half months you and Cairo have not slept together? I don't believe it. I really believe you are holding out on the tea. All that fine man and as hungry as you are, humph, I know you're lying to me."

Becca lounges across my bed as I unpack my bags from the longest trip I have taken ever. Her reaction to my truth makes me laugh. "Girl, believe it. I have been so worried about my dad, the last thing on my mind has been sex. But now that my dad is okay, and I can get back to my life, he is going to get some of this." We both laugh.

"Well, sis, I'm so happy for you. There is something I have to tell you."

Noticing the seriousness in her tone, I stop hanging clothes in the closet to look back at my friend. "What's wrong?"

"My sister has a fixation on Cairo. While you guys were in Jamaica, all hell broke loose."

"What do you mean? Your sister works for Cairo, right?"

"She does, but I'm starting to really believe she looks at him as more than her employer. And apparently, her husband thought so too. He vandalized Cairo's office, and he went to his house but got arrested as soon as he pulled up."

"Just because her cheating ass husband found a reason to point the finger at her doesn't mean anything, Becca. Come on, you know your sister better than anybody."

My friend sits up at the foot of my bed now. I try to read the expression on her face and figure out why she looks so seriously bothered.

"You're right; I do know my sister. And I have reason to believe she has a thing for Cairo. The reason I'm telling you this is because I don't want you to be surprised if she calls him after hours, or if she pops up out the blue on her off day."

My heart drops a little. During the time Cairo and I have spent together building on our friendship/relationship, I have begun to trust him. I never suspected that he has been entertaining other women while he has been spending time with me. I thought I had made it clear before we began to spend time is that I don't casually date. I date with a purpose. And my purpose will never be to be a side piece or a number two.

"Are you okay, Temp?"

Dejectedly, I respond, "Yeah, I'm okay. I just thought he was different."

"Don't do that, Temple. I didn't say he has been seeing my sister. Make no mistake about it. I just know she has been bringing him up a lot in our conversation like she's obsessed with him. She has never said he has come onto her or done anything to make her think as she does."

"How do you know?"

Becca is quiet.

"I don't. But Temple, you can't stop trusting him just because I told you my sister has a thing for him. If I thought you were going to react this way, I never would have said a word." We sit quietly for several minutes.

"Don't take it the wrong way, Temp."

"Thanks for the heads up, Becca. I'm not."

Even though I told my friend that I wasn't taking it

wrong, the dinner plans I had for us, I put them to the side. In fact, I have become guarded. So guarded that Cairo notices and he asks me what's wrong one afternoon.

"I'm okay."

"Are you sure?"

"Yes, I'm sure."

"Your energy is different, and I am worried about you."

After a few minutes of thought, I decide to be honest about the reason my energy has changed.

"My best friend's sister is your assistant."

And that is all I needed to say to get him to pour his heart out to me. First, he sits me down on his lap and gets me to look directly in his face.

"I don't know about this woman. I mean for the last five years she has been the best assistant I could ever ask for. No task was too great for her. Whatever I needed her to get done, she didn't hesitate to get it done. But then to pinpoint when she started acting crazy was right after the awards show." As he is talking to me, it looks as if he has realized something. He begins to nod his head up and down.

"Right after the awards show, she started acting weird, and so did her man. I mean, I keep trying to remember if I had ever crossed a line with her to make her think I wanted her in a romantic way and as I sit here and think the only thing I can remember is when she found out about her husband having a mistress and a new baby. She came to me crying and I took her home."

"How have you been handling knowing that she looks at you that way?"

"Well, right after we left Jamaica; it was while we were at the hospital in VA, she called me telling me that her husband was coming after me with a gun because he thought that something had been going on between us. I had him arrested the moment he drove onto my block. Then just the other day, she calls me up to tell me she wanted to check on me, because she hasn't heard from me in a while. After explaining to her that we have a work relationship that doesn't go any further than that, she didn't get it. She questioned me and I told her to take some time to find other employment. I offered to pay her another month's salary as well. Temple, I don't have time for the foolishness that she is coming with suddenly."

What he says to me goes directly with what Becca had told me. A weight is lifted from my heart because now I know he is not hiding anything from me.

"I'm sorry you had to let go of your assistant, but it probably is the best thing to you have done."

"I know. I mulled it over and over in my mind, even talked to your dad about it. I needed to make sure I wasn't being irrational with my first thought."

"You talked to my dad?"

"Yes, I talked to your dad about it."

"Wow, what did my dad have to say?"

When he finishes telling me all about the conversation between him and my dad, my panties have become so moist I could wrap my legs around him right now and tell him to take me straight to bed. I mean, don't pass go, don't worry about collecting two hundred dollars.

"Well, I'm glad everything looks like it might work out."

"And I am glad to finally see your smile again. Will you have dinner with me tomorrow night?"

"Of course. I will be there with bells on."

And I literally showed up to his door with bells sewn to my socks. Every step I took, he could hear me. With a smile, he kisses my forehead, then leads me to his large dining room. The table is set for two with two tall candles lit in the middle. It is a romantic setting many women dream of.

"Cairo, I'm not really hungry."

"No? Why didn't you bring your appetite, sweetheart?"

"I brought my appetite." He looks at me with his thick eyebrows raised, until I stand, allowing my duster to fall open, revealing the only thing I'm wearing is socks on my feet. Cairo licks his lips while closing the distance between us. He leans down, placing his lips over mine, then lifts me up so that I wrap my legs around his waist.

"Well, let me help you work up one."

Within minutes, I am laying in the middle of his bed. Cairo acts like he is partaking of his last meal. Closing my eyes to allow the pleasure to envelope me, I am glad that Ivory's room is on the other side of the house. This man has me singing high to the heavens, and I would be embarrassed if she knew it was me making the sounds that are coming from my mouth.

Cairo and I don't have dinner.

I fall asleep wrapped in his arms. At five a.m. the next morning, we are awakened to the sound of glass crashing against something. Cairo doesn't waste time jumping out of bed to his feet. He pulls his pants on quickly. When I move to follow him, he tells me to stay where I am. Now I'm worried that Stephanie's husband has come back because he couldn't get to Cairo the first time. I start to grab my phone, but then I remember that I left it downstairs in the dining room.

When there is tapping at the door, I almost jump out of my skin with fear.

"I'm sorry, he told me I needed to come in here with you." Now it is pointless for me to be embarrassed because I am sitting in the middle of her brother's bed naked.

"Don't even be embarrassed. You act like I don't know what happens between a woman and a man when they really like each other. Girl, boo."

Her comment causes me to laugh. "We need to call the police."

"They're already on the way."

And sure enough, when I look toward the window, I see the blue lights. I didn't notice, but Ivory has her phone in her hand. When it rings, she puts the call on speakerphone.

"Hey, Ro. Is everything okay?"

"Yes, it will be. Are you in my bedroom?"

"Yes."

"Can Temple hear me? Is she near you?"

"I'm right here."

"Put your clothes on and come out here."

Ivory and I look at each other. We are both filled with curiosity as to what we will see. Imagine my surprise when I see Aaron standing handcuffed against the police car.

"Aaron?"

Cairo turns to me, "So you know this dude?"

"Yes, this is my ex. You know the one from the bar the night his side piece threw a cheap drink in my face?"

"Oh yeah, I remember. Your friend is about to be arrested for trespassing on private property and vandalism of vehicles parked on my property."

When he says this, I notice the glass on the ground beside my car and the red brick laying on my front seat. "Really, Aaron?"

"So, I guess I didn't make enough money for you, you dump me for a millionaire. Damn, I feel low."

"You should feel low, you asshole! I didn't dump you because I was seeing someone else, I dumped you because you were." I begin to survey the damage to my car, but the police officer tells me not touch anything if I plan to press charges. Looking at the poor excuse for the man handcuffed in front of me, I shake my head. My father told me this dude was no good, yet I gave him my love anyhow.

"I will be pressing charges."

"Really, Temple?"

"Yes, you're a bum. Really? What guy vandalizes a woman's car several months after she tells him it's over, huh?" His chest had been puffed out at first, but now the deflation of his chest is visible as the police office instructs him to take a seat in the back of the vehicle.

"I need a statement from both of you."

Nodding my head, I accept a clipboard with a pen and paper from him. As I write, I can't help thinking of all the warning signs that I should have heeded to. When I'm done, the officer hands both Cairo and I cards with their contact information on them. Ivory asks me if I'm okay before she goes back in the house, leaving Cairo and I to survey the damage to my car.

"I'm sorry all this happened. You are always supposed to be safe when you're with me."

Not once did he question if there had been any validity in what Aaron had said about me leaving him because I had met a millionaire. He placed his arms around me.

"He didn't hurt me. Now my car, listen." Looking at the damage to the car I had been able to purchase when I made my home here.

"Don't worry about the car. You don't have to worry about anything as long as you promise me I am the one you want to be with."

Looking around me as the sun rises, I think about how many times since we have been together and watched the sunset. Now with the sun rising above our head, it signifies the new day that getting to know him has brought into my life.

"You are the one I want to be with. I wasn't sure about opening my heart to love you. But as sure as the sun has risen while we stand here right now, I can love you as long as you love me."

Cairo leans so that his forehead is touching mine, "I feel like you were sent to me. Before my mother passed away, she told me to be on the lookout for a woman with a beauty I have never seen, with a smile that signifies forever. And a woman who has a protective father that won't trust her with just anybody no matter how old she is. Temple Harris, that woman is you."

These are the words I had been waiting to hear even

though I didn't know these were the words I had been waiting to hear.

He didn't want me staying at my apartment, so I moved into the other side of his mini mansion with Ivory as my neighbor. Exactly a year after we met in Jamaica, Ivory suggests that we go to Jamaica again to commemorate the experience. And we do.

On the very first night, I was surprised by my mother and father showing up at my hotel suite. I should have known something was up then. My brothers, their wives, and Becca showed up too. Cairo and I walked along the beach just as the sun set. "You know I'm so glad I met you."

"And I'm glad I met you as well," I reply.

The next thing I know Cairo stops walking and gets down on one knee. At first, I don't realize exactly what he's doing until I look up and see my family and friends standing.

"I'm not going to make a long speech about my feelings when we first met and all that. You were there, and you had the same feeling as I did. We had some trials from the beginning, and the best thing about that has been we got through those trials. During that time, I believe we showed each other that we are capable of loving one another for years to come. So, with that being said, Temple Renee Harris, will you marry me?"

Tears sprang to my eyes; the sounds of a reggae song often played at island weddings is being played by the same live band that we heard the first time we came to Jamaica. My mother is holding her hands to her mouth as she waits for my response, and my dad nods his approval with a smile and tears in his eyes.

"Yes, Cairo Evans, I will marry you."

The cheers from my family bring more tears to my eyes as Cairo scoops me up into the air. "Go get your dress, baby. We are getting married tonight."

"Tonight?"

"If you're ready, then yes, we are getting married tonight."

Just as Becca had promised, she took care of everything that didn't have to do with the groom. She, my mother, and Ivory had picked out the perfect wedding dress, the perfect pair of sandals for me to walk along the beach to meet my groom in.

I am glad I opened my heart to receive love from this man. This self-made millionaire by the name of Cairo Evans.

The end.

Be on the look our for the story of Rebecca and Trey coming soon!!

To submit a manuscript to be considered, email us at submissions@majorkeypublishing.com

Be sure to LIKE our Major Key Publishing page on Facebook!

CPSIA information can be obtained
at www.ICGtesting.com
Printed in the USA
LVHW041730051120
670844LV00005B/1081